UNTAMED PASSION

CAT SCHIELD

For my Seven Sins Sisters: Naima Simone,
Karen Booth, Yahrah St. John, Jules Bennett,
Joss Wood and Janice Maynard

One

Oliver Lowell glared at the single word scrawled across the bottom of the birthday card. *Someday.* No signature. No "sorry I missed your birthday." Just one word that roused every demon Oliver had wrestled into submission these last eight years of sobriety.

Someday? What the hell kind of creepy message was that? A threat? A promise?

Just like everything else that reminded him of his father, receiving the gift of an expensive rod and reel had turned Oliver upside down. Too many times Vernon Lowell had promised to schedule a fishing trip only to have one thing after another take precedence. Was it any wonder that by the time Oliver entered high school the relationship between father and youngest son had soured to the point where they couldn't be in the same room together without snarling at each other?

Oliver tossed aside the card, grabbed his camera and headed out into the warmth of a Manhattan September afternoon. The acrid scent of exhaust and grumble of rushing traffic struck Oliver's senses as he paused on the sidewalk, gripped by a rare bout of indecision. Lost in a turbulent swirl of anger and resentment, he had no idea which way to turn.

Eight years earlier, he would've sought out his favorite dealer and scored something to dull his rage. Oblivion had been his best friend back then, his favorite way to cope with the loathing and self-disgust that no amount of professional success could eliminate. He'd been in his early twenties, either high or crashing, indifferent to how his behavior affected everyone around him. And then came the day when he'd decided to stop his destructive behavior. Sobriety hadn't made things any easier. In fact, his life became a whole lot worse as he had to face the consequences of his actions. Consequences he continued to address every day as he navigated negative opinions and constant temptation.

Which was why when his feet finally began to move, he strode toward the Soho Grand Hotel. He intended to remind himself that he was firmly in control of his addiction and not the other way around.

Bypassing the high ceilings and optimistic atmosphere of the Grand Bar and Lounge, Oliver made for the Club Room, with its large photos of vintage films and artfully grouped sofas and armchairs. At six in the evening, the place was nearly full, and Oliver snagged the only available table near the entrance with a direct line of sight to the bar.

A waiter approached and addressed him by name. Although Oliver never drank alcohol, today he ordered a neat whiskey instead of his usual club soda with lime. Impatience burned in his chest at the waiter's surprise. He didn't often test his control this way.

The rage that had cooled while he'd walked through the late summer evening flared once again. The emotion was a destructive, living thing in his gut that stole his energy and ability to focus. It was the source of every bad decision he'd ever made.

While he awaited the drink, Oliver sent his gaze touring the bar in a desperate search for a much-needed distraction from the all-too-familiar need for the numbness that drugs and alcohol provided. Through most of his teenage years and into his early twenties, oblivion had been his only escape from the anger that fed on his soul. Once he'd gotten clean, he'd still grappled with the rage that simmered close to the surface. During his early days of sobriety, while he'd been learning how to cope with his darker emotions, he'd still needed an escape. With controlled substances no longer an option, he'd found a new kind of addiction. Hooking up with anonymous women for a quick, down-and-dirty fix in a random hotel room, bathroom or even alley had seemed like the perfect cure for what ailed him. Yet those fleeting encounters left him empty and out of sorts.

So he'd reined in all his destructive behavior and poured his energy into something positive and healing. Something that grabbed his imagination and let him grow into a world-renown artist. Photography.

When the waiter returned with the whiskey and set it before Oliver, he scarcely noticed. His attention was fixed on the couple that had just walked past him on their way to the bar. More specifically, his interest was snagged by the willowy, graceful woman with sable hair restrained in a low, sleek knot. She looked like a model dressed for a go see in black skinny jeans, a snug black top and lightweight bomber jacket. In her three-inch ankle boots, she topped six feet, inches taller than her companion, something that must have poked at the man's ego, given his pushy handling of the woman as he directed her onto a barstool.

Oliver bristled as he noted the woman's stiff posture. Why was someone with her level of sophistication and refinement wasting her time with such a bully?

The woman balanced a model's portfolio on her lap as the man settled on her far side. Oliver had an unobstructed view of her profile. Even as he noted her sleek dark hair and almond-shaped eyes, suggesting she could be of Filipina descent, his hand moved automatically toward the bag beside him, fingers sliding around the camera inside. What stopped him from drawing it out and aiming the lens at the woman wasn't a sense of propriety but something else.

He'd taken up photography in high school, observing people, capturing their essence with his camera, taking from them without giving anything back. Once he'd turned professional, he'd snapped photographs that won him great acclaim, but he viewed these as career achievements rather than personal wins.

This woman evoked a desire to appreciate her up close, without the barrier of a camera between them. He wanted to absorb her with his fingers and drink her in with his lips. To close his eyes and listen to the patterns of her voice. But for now, Oliver settled back and let his gaze follow her every movement.

She sat without speaking, her gaze fixed on the cocktail the man had ordered for her, never once reaching for the martini glass. Meanwhile the man slammed two drinks in rapid succession, each one spurring his rudeness as he berated her. The third drink spilled as he gestured with the glass, but the woman had become stone. Yet, despite her stillness, Oliver sensed she wasn't cowed. Fury, not fear, made her cling to the portfolio on her lap.

Oliver watched their interaction in rapt fascination,

wishing he was close enough to overhear their exchange. She wore no rings on either hand, so their relationship wasn't a permanent one. Oliver was surprised how much this assumption cheered him. But a moment later, all he could feel was a sudden rush of fury as the guy slammed his drink on the bar, making the liquid slosh onto her. Not only did he not apologize as she began blotting her jeans with a napkin, but the guy got up from his stool and delivered yet another ultimatum. Both figures remained frozen while the man waited for the woman to reply. She left off drying her clothes and studied him with solemn eyes for several seconds before shaking her head. Obviously, this was not the response he'd been after, because he spat out a vicious retort and abandoned the woman where she sat.

As the man neared the exit, Oliver picked up his untouched drink and stood in time to bump into the guy. The expensive whiskey sloshed vigorously in the crystal tumbler. With a twist of his wrist, Oliver doused the man.

"What the hell?" he shouted, glaring at Oliver.

"Sorry about that." Oliver pushed sincerity into his tone, hiding his satisfaction as the bully got a little taste of his own rudeness.

"Sorry?" the man raged, pulling out a business card. "I don't care if you're sorry. I want you to pay for my dry cleaning."

"Of course." Oliver scanned the card. "Ty Littel. I promise you'll be hearing from me soon."

"It's pronounced Li-*tell*, not Little."

Oliver inclined his head and replied smoothly, "My mistake."

"Whatever." With a sneer, Littel pushed past Oliver and stomped toward the exit.

Tapping the card against his fingertips, Oliver watched until the man disappeared from sight. He then headed toward the bar and the woman who sat stiffly facing forward, her lips tight with suppressed emotion. Oliver stepped up to her side and slid a fifty toward the bartender to cover the couple's tab. He'd noted when Littel had left his date that he'd neglected to pay for the drinks.

"That guy was a dick," Oliver declared, hoping his words would alleviate some of the sting from the previous encounter. "You're better off without him."

Not wanting to intrude after what had been a fraught moment for the woman, he'd intended to make the gallant gesture and leave. But then her warm-brown gaze touched his, and for an instant, every thought came to a crashing halt. He was utterly transfixed by the emotions darting across her oval face. Anger. Horror. Recognition. Relief. The changes came so fast that Oliver could barely keep up. But it wasn't until she slammed the door on her reaction to his appearance that an elusive memory tugged at him.

"Do I know you?" The question blurted out of him.

He expected her to bristle at the obvious pickup line in a hotel bar. Instead, her left eyebrow gave a minute twitch.

"Do I look familiar?"

"Somewhat. I just can't place you. Are you a model?"

Her lashes flickered, giving the impression that his question displeased her. "For the moment."

Her enigmatic remark stirred his curiosity. "I thought so. I'm Oliver Lowell."

A tiny tug at the corner of her mouth might have indicated a smile. "I know."

Unsurprising, since he'd made a splash in the fashion industry as a model before earning a solid reputation around town for his photography. "Have I photographed you?"

When he'd quit modeling, the transition to fashion photography had made the most sense. He'd started by doing beauty shots for up-and-coming models, and his work had been so well received that he'd started getting offers from magazines.

She shook her head.

"Of course not," he murmured. "I definitely would've remembered you."

Her enigmatic smile flashed, making his fingers twitch, but as before, not in the direction of his camera. He longed to caress her flawless skin and see if it could possibly be as soft and smooth as it appeared.

"So, where did our paths cross?" he asked, scouring his memories but finding only a vague impression that they'd met. Not surprising, since much of his early twenties were lost in a drug-induced haze.

"We walked the Valentino spring show eight years ago." As they spoke, she eased the white-knuckle grip on the purse in her lap. Now she brushed a wayward curl behind her ear with long fingers, tipped with short nails painted a forgettable nude. "It was my first runway show."

Fury and self-loathing burned in Oliver's gut. "And my last."

That was the night his friend died from an overdose. A night where Oliver had not been there for Carson because he'd been too busy screwing up his life.

"And now you're behind the lens," she said, seemingly unaware that his thoughts had taken him down a dark road. "How does that feel?"

"I like being in control," he replied, ignoring the mocking laughter echoing in the back of his mind.

Control was something he hadn't known much growing up as the youngest son of a powerful family. His father had pushed him to do better, to match the achievements of his older twin brothers, and then punished Oliver when he failed to live up to the expectations established by Joshua and Jacob.

He'd had no control when his father told him he would attend Falling Brook Prep and later Harvard. Nor when Oliver had tried to resist his father's heavy hand and join the photography club. Older brother Joshua's artistic talent and their mother's insistence on indulging it, despite their father's protests, meant that Oliver had been bullied into going out for soccer and baseball.

Nor had he been in control at Harvard. The circumstances surrounding his father's disappearance led him to act out. Partying and doing drugs had been a deep dive into his anger that his father had abandoned them all.

"Control," she murmured, her bitter tone deepening Oliver's fascination. "What's that like?"

Control was choice. He'd learned in therapy that everyone responded differently to pressure. Josh had chosen responsibility. Jacob decided to retreat. Oliver's refuge had been oblivion. Until rehab had taught him a different way to cope.

"I like being in charge."

Her eyes narrowed in speculation. "I imagine you do."

He considered the scene between her and the man who'd left. "You should try it."

"Maybe I should." She swiveled on the stool, facing him. "How do I start?"

"You might start by dumping the boyfriend."

"Too late." Her gaze rolled toward the exit. "He already gave me the heave-ho."

Oliver greeted the bit of news with a nod while satisfaction fired in his chest. His mood was lightening with each passing second in her company. "His loss is my gain."

Her eyes widened in surprise at his blunt statement, but she made no move to shut him down.

"Earlier you said you're a model *for now*," he continued,

eager to learn more about what made her tick. "Are you thinking of quitting?"

"I've been modeling since I was one year old. Twenty-five years in the business is long enough, don't you think?"

"I wouldn't know," he admitted. "I only modeled for five."

"And quit at the top of your game," she pointed out. "How come?"

"Always go out with a bang," he quipped, before thinking the better of his answer. This woman was contemplating a major life change and deserved better than a flippant reply. "If I kept going with modeling, I'd be dead."

Rather than shock her, his stark declaration caused her to nod. "It really is a terrible business," she said in complete seriousness. "Why do so many want to break in?"

He wanted to banish the shadows filling her eyes. Their presence hinted at a painful history.

"Obviously for the fast and easy money," he said, dark amusement lightening his tone.

"And the short hours," she added, the corners of her lips twitching into a semblance of a smile.

"And of course," he added, recalling hundreds of rejections that followed hours and hours spent in casting calls, auditions and go-sees, "the self-esteem boost."

She dipped her head in recognition. "Nothing like being regarded like a piece of meat."

They both took a second to absorb the words, and Oliver found himself in sync with someone for the first time in more years than he could count. A second later he noticed that his earlier anger was gone. Conversing with this woman was the distraction he'd been looking for.

"So, if you're not planning to model in the future, what do you want to do instead?"

"I don't know," she admitted, looking crestfallen. "And until I have a plan, I can't stop modeling."

The same desire that had prompted him to dump a drink on her date and pay her bar tab swept through him now. Having little patience for weakness, he'd never championed anyone before. He had no explanation for why now and why this woman except that since she'd entered the bar, his mood had improved, and he didn't want the distraction to end.

"Maybe I can help."

The wild pounding of Sammi Guzman's heart drove the breath from her body. She gaped at Oliver Lowell, astonished how readily her teenage crush flared back to life.

And yet, was it really a surprise? In snug jeans, a white T-shirt and worn bomber jacket, the man exuded raw male charisma and swoon-worthy sex appeal. She'd been more than a little giddy since he'd sat down beside her at the bar. Now, with his penetrating gaze fixed on her, all sorts of reckless urges were awakening.

"Help how?" she wheezed out, unable to believe her luck.

"Let me take your picture."

Disappointed, she said the first thing that popped into her head. "Oh."

"Oh?" he echoed, a muscle jumping in his square jaw.

Convinced she'd insulted him, Sammi smiled to soften the rebuff. "That's not at all what I expected you to say, and I'm flattered that the incredibly talented Oliver Lowell wants to photograph me, but I'm looking to escape my modeling career, not turn up the heat on it."

Long moments passed while he pondered her response in grim silence. She fiddled with the untouched martini Ty had ordered while her nerves jangled and her thoughts raced. The last time she and Oliver had occupied the same room, she'd been seventeen and he hadn't known she was alive. In the eight years since, he'd added muscle to his tall frame, changing from a willful pretty boy with an aggressive stare and petulant mouth into a gorgeous hunk with guarded eyes and a commanding presence. One thing that hadn't changed was his reputation for brilliance and a volatile temper.

"This will be a photo just between us."

His enigmatic words scrambled her emotions. She didn't understand his interest in her. For months and months after walking in the same runway show, she'd imagined a different sort of encounter with Oliver, where his penetrating blue eyes wouldn't look past her or through her, but where she would have his full attention. She'd indulged romantic daydreams where he swept her off her feet and overwhelmed her with soul-stealing kisses.

Of course, nothing like that could ever have happened. Even if Oliver had been interested in her, Sammi's freedom was limited by her mother. A reckless thrill spurred her racing pulse to greater speed. Although Celeste hadn't relinquished her influence over her daughter, Sammi was no longer a child.

"Is this your version of come up and see my etchings?" she asked, wincing at the awkwardness of her banter.

He arched his left eyebrow, the one split in half by a scar. Far from taking away from the perfection of his face, the flaw enhanced his appeal.

"No," he said, even as something hot and unsettling flared in his eyes for the briefest of seconds. "This is a legitimate offer."

"So this isn't some elaborate come-on?"

He blinked in surprise. From his startled reaction to her question, she'd read his invitation all wrong. Mortified heat stung her cheeks as she contemplated the bad impression he must have of her. First, he'd seen her badgered and then abandoned by Ty. Now she was misunderstanding his offer to help her.

"Maybe I should explain what I'm talking about."

"That would be great," she murmured, determined to stop making a fool of herself.

"What I love about being a photographer is how I get to see the world through the lens of my imagination." Oliver began his explanation slowly, his gaze directed toward the rows of bottles behind the bar, but his attention was turned inward. "After I quit modeling, I went back to what I'd loved to do when I was still in high school." His features went as still as stone as he reflected on his past. "Initially I started with what I knew, but being a fashion photographer was nearly as boring as being a model. But I needed to eat, so I took the jobs that came my way. To supplement my income I also helped up-and-coming models build their portfolios. It was in those portrait sessions that I discovered my true passion. And those photos led to my work being noticed. Suddenly I was in demand, with offers from magazines to shoot celebrities and other people of note."

Oliver paused in his story and shook free of his past. He raked the long fingers of his left hand through his wavy dark blond hair and suddenly seemed younger than his thirty-two years.

"While celebrities are accustomed to being photographed, they wear their public personas like a mask. I became interested in what made them tick."

"And did you find out?"

"It often took a long time. I took thousands of photos in a session and often wore them down to the point of exhaustion. It becomes difficult to maintain a facade as the mind grows tired." From the expression on his face, he'd gone to a moment far away from this hotel bar. "The photos I took in the minutes after we wrapped were sometimes the most fascinating pictures of the day. But they weren't magazine quality. They were for me and my subjects."

His deep voice had drawn her into his tale, and she caught herself leaning forward to catch his every word. Shocked to realize she'd dropped her guard, Sammi straightened her spine. Her breath gave a little hitch as her retreat caused his gaze to glance off hers.

Wondering what he'd glimpsed in her eyes, Sammi cleared her throat. "So you showed them the photos?"

"I print one, something that captured their essence and revealed their true nature, and deliver it." Oliver sounded as indifferent as if he discussed the weather. "It's up to them to decide what to do with the picture."

Sammi shivered as a fanciful notion took root. Some cultures believed that taking a person's photograph was like stealing their soul. For someone who'd spent her life in front of a camera, she'd always kept her emotions hidden and portrayed what the client wanted to see. She'd never observed a single image of herself that came close to exposing all she was.

What would Oliver Lowell lay bare?

"Having your greatest vulnerability captured..." Sammi shuddered. "That sounds terrifying."

He nodded in understanding. "For some it can be."

Sammi thought this sounded presumptuous of him. No doubt growing up in an affluent family left him indifferent to what others might struggle with. Through this entire encounter her perception of Oliver had been shifting. At first, she'd been thrilled that her teenage crush had finally noticed her, but she was fast discovering that he possessed more layers than she'd imagined.

"So, what do you say?" he prompted, breaking into her troubled thoughts.

"About?"

"Letting me take your photo?"

Sammi thought about the difficult evening that stretched before her once she returned to the apartment she shared with her mother. Explaining that Ty had broken up with her would result in a lengthy lecture on her foolishness. Celeste was obsessed with financial security and saw her daughter's relationship with a successful ad executive as a positive thing. In fact, without her mother's pushing, Sammi would have ended things with Ty long before his resentment had led him to grow abusive.

"I don't know," she hedged, conscious that she'd already made her decision.

"You can trust me."

And in a moment of sudden and shocking clarity, Sammi realized she did. "It occurred to me that I probably can't afford what you normally charge to photograph people. Just out of curiosity, what do you charge for these private portrait sessions?"

"Usually a hundred thousand dollars."

"Seriously?" She gaped at him. "No offense, but why are people willing to pay so much?"

"Privacy." He spoke matter-of-factly. "I show them something no one else has captured before. Something they might not wish the world to see." His self-assurance hummed like a high-voltage wire. Get too close to this man and it might prove fatal. "They are paying for my integrity. No picture I take of them will never find its way into the public domain unless they choose to release it."

She gusted out a breath. "Well, I guess that means that this photo shoot isn't going to happen, because I don't have a hundred thousand dollars to give you."

"I didn't expect you did." He gestured toward her purse. "How much money do you have with you?"

"Let's see." Sammi pulled out her wallet. "Twenty-three dollars." She pulled out the bills and flashed them.

Oliver plucked the bills from her hand and stuffed them into his jacket pocket. "Then for twenty-three dollars, I will take one picture of you."

"Photographers take hundreds to get the perfect shot," she said, knowing he was doing her a favor but unable to stop herself from pushing back. Earlier when he'd spoken of capturing the essence of his subjects, she'd been both intrigued and filled with skepticism. Most people guarded their true selves and reluctantly gave up their dark secrets to their shrinks, much less allowed them to be exposed to a camera. "You're going to do it in one try?"

"Are you challenging my ability as a photographer?"

Understanding dawned. This was the game he played. The challenge that he set for himself with each new client. It wasn't enough for him to take amazing photographs for magazines. He had to do something that proved he was a master of his craft.

If Oliver seemed annoyed by her continued resistance, he gave no sign. They relocated to a cozy couch in the Grand Bar and Lounge, where Oliver ordered a sampling of small plates and a club soda for himself. Determined to keep a clear head, Sammi followed suit. While they ate, Oliver shared stories of the celebrities he'd photographed, and Sammi described her modeling experiences overseas.

He watched her with rapt focus. Not like a predator, preparing to pounce, but as if she was some rarity and he an avid collector.

"What?" she demanded, equal parts intrigued and terrified beneath his curious stare.

Was she imagining that something was happening between them? She no longer believed his sole purpose in approaching her had been to get her into bed. His mysterious behavior made him impossible to read, and that only enhanced his sex appeal. She wanted to be alone with him, to immerse herself in his kisses and let her body be in control for a change.

Something must've shown in her expression, because he leaned forward to whisper in her ear.

"I find you fascinating."

The remark…the confession…or maybe the awe in his voice set her on fire. What had once been a teenager's unrequited crush became the beginnings of a woman's full-blown obsession.

The air around her grew too thin to breathe. Dizzy, she gripped the sleeve of his leather jacket to steady herself as his warm breath feathered across her cheek. She was on the verge of turning her head and meeting the lips that hovered so near, when he eased back. But even as disappointment flowed into her, Oliver stood and extended his hand to her.

"Let's get out of here." There was both command and entreaty in his tone.

"Where to?" Seized by something momentous and exhilarating, she grasped his long fingers and let him draw her to her feet.

"You paid me for a photo." His deep voice rumbled through her. "It's time I deliver."

Neither spoke as they exited the hotel and strolled along the sidewalk. Sammi settled her hands deep into her coat pockets and resisted the urge to take his arm. She wasn't accustomed to initiating spontaneous acts of affection. As Sammi grew up, her mother had often treated her more like a client than a daughter, claiming Sammi needed to develop a thick skin if she was going to survive in the fashion industry.

He escorted her into a building several blocks from the hotel and directed her toward the elevator. As the car rose,

Sammi's nerves begin to buzz like an angry hive of wasps. By the time the doors opened on the eighth floor, anxiety had completely overwhelmed the feverish attraction that had compelled her to accompany Oliver Lowell to his SoHo loft. What was she doing here? Yet she didn't flee as he unlocked a door and gestured her inside. Instead, she hid her uneasiness behind a polite, practice smile, and entered the space.

Fifteen hundred square feet of open loft greeted her, looking similar to every photography studio she'd ever worked in. She surveyed the industrial vibe of the place, gaze roaming over brick walls interspersed with large windows, bleached-white walls and gleaming wood floors. The only furnishings were a couple of couches and some worktables. She spied computers, lighting equipment and a white screen.

Sammi exhaled, releasing the tension she hadn't realized she was holding. "This is your studio," she said, surprise in her voice even as disappointment hung like a stone in her chest.

"Were you expecting something else?" He arched that sexy split eyebrow and made her heart flutter.

"When we first entered the building, I thought maybe you lived here."

"I do. Upstairs." He indicated an open staircase off to the left. "Do you want a tour?"

The offer astounded her. Given how little was known of his private life, she guessed he guarded his privacy zealously. Should she feel honored that he'd offered her a glimpse? But at what price?

"Maybe later."

Turning her back to him, she set her portfolio and purse on a nearby table and stripped off her jacket while she sorted through her conflicting moods. What had seemed like a daring lark at the Soho Grand Hotel no longer felt inconsequential.

"Although I'm sure your mind is racing," Oliver said, "I can't for the life of me tell what you're thinking."

That I'm completely out of my depth with you.

Sammi trembled as he strolled toward the worktable that held the cameras. What would he see? What would she betray of herself? Her inner turmoil? Her failures? All her life she'd taken for granted that she was beautiful. When he cracked her psyche and exposed her soul, would she be ugly? What could possibly be more terrifying? She wondered how many of his photographs existed. How many people were strong enough to keep a visual representation of their greatest failures and most shameful secrets?

It was a struggle to keep from rubbing at the goose bumps on her arms. "Where do you want me?" she asked, needing to get this over before her courage failed.

"Where would you feel most comfortable?"

She didn't hesitate before striding toward the white screen. After twenty-five years there was nowhere she felt more at home than on set. Here, she became a girl next door, a seductress, a woman in love, a rag doll, a warrior, a free spirit, a crusader. Or any one of a thousand other incarnations. Finding the center of the backdrop, she turned to face Oliver and found him watching her, his right hand resting on a camera, as if halted amid the act of picking it up.

"How do you get people to open up so that you can photograph them stripped down to their essence?"

"It's different for every person. The key is to find the trigger that allows their guard to fall."

"How do you make that happen?" While Sammi never hesitated when asked to pose in the nude, contemplating the exposure of her inner landscape made her woozy with anxiety. "How do you break down their walls?"

"Before the subject comes in to be photographed, I do a significant amount of research on them."

"What sort of research?"

"Background on their personal and professional lives."

Sammi shivered as she considered what her complicated relationship with her mother revealed about her. "I imagine you know exactly what to say to bring up all sorts of negative feelings."

The way his expression hardened to stone at her remark told her she'd made a misstep.

"I'm not trying to hurt anyone," he said at last, his flat tone not quite hiding his strong emotions. "The photoshoot isn't successful if the client is unhappy."

"That makes sense," Sammi murmured. "So how do you use the information you gather?"

"I ask questions, get them to talk about pivotal moments in their lives."

"What would you ask me?"

To her surprise he came away empty-handed from the table of camera equipment. "Why do you want to do this?"

"I want to see what you see when you look at me."

As good as he was at controlling his facial expressions, her answer had obviously surprised him.

"Why do you care how I see you?"

"Because you make me feel…"

She moved in his direction, keen desire driving away common sense. She'd dated Ty for six months and never once slept with him, yet tonight she'd gone home with a virtual stranger, proving she wasn't the frigid bitch he'd accused her of being.

"How do I make you feel?" Oliver prompted, hunger intensifying the bold blue of his eyes.

Lust tightened deep in her belly as she tunneled her fingertips beneath his bomber. Riding the hard muscles of his chest and upper arms, she slid the jacket off his broad shoulders and let it fall to the floor.

His strong fingers fanned over her hips, drawing her firmly against his hard planes. A hot ache flared between her thighs as her lower half settled against his. The hard thrust of his growing erection bumped against her as Oliver's lips grazed along her neck. With a moan she tipped her head to the side and pressed her breasts into his hard chest, communicating her sharp need. Where she half expected anxiousness or doubts to surface, Sammi knew only the enticing shimmer of anticipation rising inside her.

"That tour you offered me earlier," she said, one hand gliding beneath the hem of his T-shirt and discovering the hot silk of his skin while the fingers of her other hand raked into his thick hair. "I'm ready to take it."

Two

Her lips were impossibly soft beneath his, and Oliver lingered over their pliant sweetness for several heartbeats until she tilted her head and gave a low whimper. He hummed in pleasure even as he offered her one last opportunity to snatch at reason.

Instead, she dug her fingertips into his back, showing that her hunger matched his, and Oliver shifted closer still, claiming her lips, taking the breath she surrendered. He pushed his tongue into her mouth as need descended on him. Lashed by urgency, lost in the howling lust the kiss unleashed, he pinned her body against his and took everything she offered and more.

Oliver woke with a start, jarred awake by the insistent bleat of his smartphone. Muttering curses, he set his jaw against the shocking ache in his loins and rolled over. As he went to snatch the phone off the nightstand, it slid onto the floor under his bed. Hauling it up by the charging cable, he disconnected the power with a ruthless jerk and answered.

"What?"

"Your shoot at EW starts in an hour." The soothing female voice on the other end of the call belonged to his assistant. "The car will be downstairs in twenty minutes."

"Fine." All too aware that he'd overslept, Oliver hung up without thanking her for keeping him on schedule. It wouldn't do his reputation any favors to show up late to a photoshoot.

Following a quick shower, Oliver dressed in faded jeans and a gray T-shirt. Snatching up one of his numerous leather jackets, he slid his feet into his favorite black suede sneakers and headed for the front door.

Heidi met him in the lobby with a cup of coffee and a pair of sunglasses. He accepted both before pushing through his building's front doors. Outside, a crisp mid-October morning slammed into his senses with the decaying scent of dying greenery and the bite of early frost. Morning sunlight slanted over the facade of his building, the lower angle another indication of the passage of the seasons. Oliver slid on the dark glasses, all too aware that he was on the verge of brooding all through October in the same way he'd done with the latter weeks of September.

Time was rushing by while Oliver wallowed in a bog of bad moods and fuming. Not only had the sender of the fishing equipment remained anonymous, but also he couldn't find the woman he'd spent the night with six weeks earlier. As soon as that encounter popped into his mind, a memory of the following morning rose to torment him. After a night of amazing sex, he'd awakened to find himself alone in his big bed and his apartment empty. As unsatisfying as that had been, that they had unfinished business made her vanishing act that much harder to move on from.

Making no effort to stifle his ever-present frustration, Oliver stormed past the black-clad driver and slid into the back seat of the awaiting town car. He balanced the to-go cup on his knee and glared out the window as Heidi slid into the passenger seat in front of him and the driver took his place behind the wheel.

He hated to be this preoccupied with a woman he barely knew, even though they'd slept together. Especially when his prime reason for inviting her back to his studio and offering to photograph her was because he'd needed a distraction that night. Sure, Suzi fascinated him and he'd been curious to find out why she reacted the way she had to her boyfriend's poor treatment. Or maybe he'd been drawn in because she'd been at the last runway show he ever participated in. Despite the fact that his recall of that night was hazy, the event marked a major turning point in his life.

When the evening had played out differently than he'd planned, Oliver was content to let a different sort of distraction consume him. He'd assumed that after they each satisfied their appetite for each other, he would have a better idea of what made her tick and could produce the promised photograph. He discovered, however, that his desire for her was stronger than his curiosity. They'd made love through the night, before falling asleep in the wee hours. He remembered gathering her into his arms, nuzzling his face into the crook of her neck and drifting in profound contentment in the moments before he dropped off.

Most women he slept with liked to stick around. Sex relaxed him, allowing him to revel in the moment and put all his energy into satisfying whoever occupied his bed. Never in a million years had he expected that after the sexual connection he and Suzi had made that she'd vanish before he awoke. Worse, as bright morning sunlight flooded his loft, he'd realized he had no idea her last name or how to get ahold of her. Since he'd given her his business card with his private number on the back, he'd assumed she'd call. But when several days went by without contact, he'd decided to go on the offensive and tasked his assistant to find a Filipina model with the first name Suzi.

Heidi hadn't been the least bit surprised by his request. As his assistant, she was accustomed to doing all sorts of tasks for him, and finding a model was hardly unusual. But when she'd come up empty, his excessive surliness had been noteworthy.

At five minutes before ten, he strode into the workroom at EW Lingerie and surveyed the scene. His team had everything ready for the shoot. His photography assistant had set up the lighting per his instructions. He glanced toward the corner where racks of cotton, silk and lace undergarments waited beside the hair and makeup tables. Instead of hiring professional models for the shoot, the designers of the inclusive underwear brand were to be highlighted wearing their lingerie. The magazine had chosen to feature EW Lingerie—the initials standing for Every Woman—because the brand had been created by three women with a mission to bring affordable lingerie to women of all shapes and sizes without sacrificing beauty, style or comfort.

A camera was placed in Oliver's outstretched hand as he approached the set. With an effort of will, he shoved aside all distraction and focused on what he was being paid big bucks to do. He expected a difficult shoot based on the fact that he wasn't working with professional models, and many women wouldn't be comfortable posing in their underwear. He was therefore delighted that the three owners were eager to have some fun and proud of their product.

After snapping several hundred photos with numerous wardrobe changes, Oliver shifted out of artist mode and noticed the room's energy had changed. Accustomed to being the center of attention, Oliver sensed he was receiving a different sort of interest. Setting down his camera, he caught Heidi's eye and waved her over.

"What's going on?" he asked, noting that his team was making an effort to avoid looking his way.

"Everything went smoothly," Heidi declared with a bright smile. "The magazine is going to love the images."

Convinced she was hiding something, Oliver settled a hard glare on her. "I'm not talking about the shoot. I know that went well." He narrowed his eyes at the anxious energy surrounding him. Something was wrong. "So, I'm going to ask you again, and this time you're going to give me a straight answer. What's going on?"

"There's been some news." She paused, looking like she wanted to be anywhere but standing in front of him at the moment. "It's about your family."

Suddenly Oliver understood why everybody was treating him like an escaped wild animal. They were afraid to set him off. He ground his teeth in irritation. It was one thing for him to terrorize his crew when something went wrong on set. It was something else for them to tiptoe around him because of his personal issues. Restraining a growl, Oliver strode to where he left his leather jacket. He scooped it up, feeling the weight of his silenced smartphone in the left pocket. Without a word to anyone, he headed out.

Oliver's phone was in his hands and his fingers were typing *Black Crescent* into the search bar before the elevator reached the ground floor. His long legs carried him to the sidewalk as the first news article materialized on the screen.

Vernon Lowell Lives! Black Crescent Fugitive Located in Remote Caribbean Location.

His father was...alive.

The shock of it hit Oliver's psyche like a hundred-foot tsunami wave, sending his emotions spinning, scrambling his thoughts. The air around him grew heavy. It was as if he floundered beneath the surface of the ocean with no sense of up or down. Unable to breathe, Oliver stumbled toward the nearest solid object and placed his shoulder against the building's concrete facade.

That damned fishing pole. It had come from his father after all.

As this realization seared across his brain, fury replaced his initial shock. With acid burning his gut raw, Oliver scanned the bombshell article splashed all over the national news. Vernon Lowell had been spotted on a remote Caribbean island. For fifteen years Vernon had been in hiding, enjoying his life on a Caribbean island while his family faced all the public scrutiny and ridicule. Oliver gripped his smartphone until his fingers turned white.

How could this be happening? His father was alive?

With a curse, Oliver hurled his phone into the Manhattan traffic. Overcome with need to find a bar and demand a shot of whiskey, he started walking. No, not a shot, an entire bottle. Only oblivion would let him escape the rush of powerful emotion filling him. He moved toward the curb and hailed a cab, directing the driver to take him to the Soho Grand Hotel. Then, thoughts churning, he collapsed against the seat and stared unseeing out the window as Manhattan slid past.

When the taxi stopped outside the hotel, Oliver passed the fare to the driver. With his wallet still in his hand, he exited the vehicle. Oliver started toward the hotel's front door and then stopped. Of their own volition, his fingers wrapped around the stainless dog tags dangling around his neck. Tightening his fist around the talismans, Oliver focused on calming his unsteady breathing.

The necklace bore two dog tags, one his own, the other belonging to Carson Bowles, Oliver's best friend. The two buddies had been all sorts of bad as they drank and partied their nights away. They'd started out modeling around the same time and bought the matching necklaces after walking their first New York Fashion Week runway. Superstitious about the dog tags, they never went anywhere without them, taking them off only to work. As lucky charms, the necklaces proved their effectiveness over and over. Was it any wonder that the night Carson left his behind at the last runway show either of them ever worked was the night he died?

Oliver often wondered if he'd made more of an effort to find his friend that night if Carson would still be alive. That night had started out like most others. Oliver had hit a couple of clubs, partied with some people he knew, but never caught up with his friend. After running out of drugs, Oliver had been looking to score. Unable to get ahold of his regular source, he'd met up with a dealer he didn't know. Drunk as hell and high on something a lot more potent than life, he'd ended up badly beaten. While he was recovering, Oliver found out Carson had overdosed.

His family never visited him at the hospital, nor stepped in to ease his legal troubles. Not surprising, since they'd abandoned him long before he'd made a mess of his life. So when he ended up in court-appointed rehab, he had only a gutful of regret and his best friend's necklace to get him through the worst days.

And as Oliver turned away from the hotel, resisting the urge to drink himself into darkness, the dog tag, engraved with Carson's name and the date he'd died, saved him from making a huge mistake now.

Sammi gazed out the window of the two-bedroom Manhattan apartment she shared with her mother and worried Oliver's business card between her fingers. The once sharp edges of the heavy paper had grown soft from handling. At least once a day Sammi took out the card and ran her fingers over the embossed front before turning the card over and staring at the ten numbers written in Oliver's bold script.

In the early days following their night together, she'd been tempted to program his contact information into her phone. She'd reasoned that their unforgettable night together could be the start of something blissful and amazing. But as the days turned into weeks, time and distance put her bubblegum daydreams into perspective. Oliver Lowell wasn't a teenage girl's dashing hero but a complicated man with anger issues and no track record of lasting relationships.

That's why she'd crept out of his SoHo loft at dawn six weeks earlier without saying goodbye and why she'd never called. As to why she couldn't bring herself to throw away his number…

She could say she'd kept the business card because he owed her a photo. A single portrait of her that she'd paid twenty-three dollars for. Even though she could afford to walk away from the paltry sum, a thrill that was half terror and half delight danced down her spine at the thought of demanding that he honor their verbal contract and give her what he promised. Sammi knew she'd never go through with it. What use did she have for an image of herself that exposed her soul?

Absolutely none.

Which brought her to this moment and a whole new purpose for reaching out to Oliver.

"What do you mean you're quitting modeling?" her mother demanded. She threw her arm wide to indicate the gorgeous apartment with stunning views. "How are we going to afford this if you quit?"

"*We* are not," Sammi said, her voice cracking beneath a burden of exhaustion and worry.

In the two weeks since the pregnancy test had been positive, she'd been overwhelmed by pregnancy hormones and anxiety about the future. Tired all the time and brought low by morning sickness, Sammi found herself paralyzed about the changes rushing at her. All she wanted to do was curl up in her bed and shut out the world. But her mother's expectations drove her relentlessly.

Celeste frowned. "Then where do you think we're going to go?"

"I don't know where *you* are going to go," she said, cringing away from her mother's dismay, hating the guilt that flared at her mother's fear. For years Celeste had been a drain on Sammi's finances. Why couldn't she be at peace about cutting ties? "*I'm* going to move somewhere I can afford."

The thought of living on her own filled Sammi with a perplexing mixture of relief and dismay. Her mother had been with her all her life, directing Sammi's career, pushing her to work harder, interfering in her daughter's personal life until Sammi wasn't sure she could succeed on her own. Frustrated by such unwelcome doubts, she shoved all emotion aside and focused on dealing with her mother's escalating dissatisfaction.

"Somewhere you can afford?" Celeste demanded. "What about me? What am I supposed to do?" As fast as a snake could strike, Celeste's tone went from outrage to self-pity. "Have you thought about me at all?"

"I have."

In fact, Sammi had thought a great deal about her mother. About how Celeste had pushed her daughter into an industry before she was a year old. An industry that had defined her worth by how she appeared. Sammi wasn't a top model in New York—although she'd had a great deal of success overseas—but by working her ass off, she had a significant income. Money that supported her mother in style. A mother who'd emigrated from the Philippines because she wanted a different life for her daughter. A mother who'd capitalized on that daughter's beauty and was now reaping the benefits of Sammi's success with a comfortable Manhattan apartment and luxurious lifestyle.

"I don't believe you," Celeste snarled. "This is just like you to jump before you've thought everything through."

Sammi wished she had snappy answers to give to her mother, a definite plan all worked out. It was just that she so rarely got to think for herself.

"Just because I don't have all the answers doesn't mean I haven't given this a great deal of thought."

Noting her daughter's defensive stance, Celeste's gaze narrowed, and she capitalized on Sammi's uncertainty. "Well, you should just continue modeling while you figure it out."

Why? Because Sammi had wanted to figure out what she would do with the rest of her life when modeling was no longer an option, but her mother never gave her the breathing room to do so. It would be no different now.

"Because I don't have time," Sammi said.

"What do you mean you don't have time?" Her mother waved her hand dismissively. "You're twenty-six, for heaven's sake. Xiao Wen Ju wasn't even discovered until her twenties." Celeste often bullied her daughter by referencing non-Caucasian top models. "If you worked as hard as she did, you might land on the cover of *Vogue* or be signed as the face of a top designer. Until then you can still walk the runway."

Sammi shoved aside her anxiety and focused on irritation. Her mother never stopped badgering her about working. Well, at least that was at an end.

"I'm pregnant." She braced herself for her mother's explosion, but what came next shocked her even more.

"Oh, is that all?"

"Is that all?" Sammi echoed. How could her mother be so blasé about something so momentous?

"You can take care of that in an afternoon."

Sammi recoiled. "Take care of…?" As in terminate the pregnancy? Tears sprang to her eyes at Celeste's insensitivity. She'd barely taken a moment before dismissing what the pregnancy might mean to Sammi. A second later the acid burn of resentment flared in her stomach. Or maybe it was the crackers she'd eaten earlier intending to make a reappearance. "I'm not *taking care of* anything."

Her mother's almond-shaped eyes went nearly round with astonishment. "You can't possibly mean to go through with the pregnancy?" After a second she gave a scornful half laugh. "You're such a foolish child. Do you have any idea the sacrifices being a mother requires?"

Do you?

The question demanded release, but Sammi didn't dare voice it for fear that once she ventured down that path, she'd say things that would cause irreparable harm. As focused and stubborn as her mother could be, she was all the family Sammi had. Without her mother, Sammi would be all alone. The thought terrified her.

"How will you support yourself?" Celeste demanded when Sammi remained lost in her thoughts.

"I'll find a job."

"A job?" her mother scoffed. "Doing what? You don't know how to do anything but pose in front of the camera."

The harsh truth made Sammi wince. While this was true, she couldn't believe that this was the limit of her abilities. She'd never had the opportunity to explore anything other than modeling. What could she do? What did she want to do?

"That's not all I can do. I will start at the bottom."

"You can't seriously expect to start from the bottom and be able to support yourself in Manhattan?"

"So maybe I don't stay here," Sammi said, fear making her breathless. Aside from the five years she'd spent modeling overseas, she'd never lived anywhere but New York City. She didn't know how to drive a car or what might await her outside the fashion industry.

Her mother's mocking laughter rang in her ears. "I didn't raise my daughter to be a fool. Don't be one now."

"I'm not a fool," Sammi said, clamping her teeth together as bile rose in her throat.

What if her mother was right about everything? Did she seriously think she could raise a child on her own without modeling? What could she do to make money? Swamped by uncertainty and fear, Sammi headed for the front door. More than anything she needed to clear her head.

"Where are you going?" her mother shrieked after her.

"Out."

She was on the street and signaling a cab before she had any sense of where she intended to go. Not until she settled into the back seat, and the man asked for an address, did she give into the tears she'd been holding back. Where was she going to go? Who could she turn to for help? All her friends were models. It was likely their advice would be no different from her mother's recommendations. Celeste jealously guarded her influence over Sammi, blocking anyone else who might have offered career counseling.

Sammi gave the driver the address of her modeling agency. She needed to have a conversation with them about her condition and take that first step into her future. If they fired her on the spot, it would certainly galvanize her to make a plan. As she dashed away her tears, Sammi realized she still held Oliver's card in her hand. That was another difficult conversation she needed to have. Yet for some reason it was the one she was least afraid of.

Before they'd gone more than a few blocks, she directed the cab to the new destination and asked him to let her out two blocks from Oliver's loft. The walk would afford her a few minutes to make up her mind about what she intended to say. She turned the card over and eyed his personal cell phone number. Should she call first? What if he avoided her call? Or refused to see her? He hadn't asked for her number that night, so obviously he had no interest in pursuing her.

Sammi's steps faltered as she approached the final intersection. Ahead, she could see Oliver's building. She looked up to the top floor, wondering if he was even there. Her mouth went desert dry. Was she really going to ambush him with her pregnancy? Would he believe her? Or would he assume she was trying to manipulate him? She could see how his elusiveness might make women desperate.

And what if Oliver Lowell was a terrible father for her child? No matter how amazing the sex or the connection she felt toward him, the fact of the matter was she didn't know anything about him, and his reputation for being temperamental and difficult worried her.

The traffic light changed twice while she stood rooted to the sidewalk.

What harm would it do if she just walked away and never told him he was going to be a father? Sammi considered how much she'd hated growing up not knowing who her dad was. She didn't even know if he knew about her, because Celeste refused to discuss him at all. That had never been fair. Somewhere she had a whole other family she'd never get to know.

Could she do that to her child?

Her feet were moving before she was even aware that the light had changed. It wasn't wise to be distracted while walking along a New York City sidewalk, but lately she found herself all too often caught up in her own thoughts and oblivious to her surroundings.

She approached Oliver's building, his card clutched in her hand, and stopped ten feet from the entrance. Frozen with indecision, she stared at the door through which she'd passed with Oliver six weeks earlier and dreaded the conversation to come. He surely wouldn't welcome the news she brought. He'd be upset. Angry. How could he not be? She was about to change his life and not for the better.

Lifting her phone, she dialed Oliver's number from memory. As the phone rang, her courage began to fail her. Her thumb started to move across the screen toward the end call button when someone picked up.

"Oliver Lowell's phone."

Sammi was so startled by the feminine voice that she hung up. Confused fragments of thought tumbled around in her brain for several seconds until she lifted Oliver's business card and compared the numbers. Only when she'd confirmed that she'd dialed correctly did she recall how the woman had answered the phone.

Her phone came to life with Oliver's number. Cursing, she stared at the screen, wondering what to do.

"Hello?"

"We got disconnected," said the woman who'd answered the moment before. "Are you looking for Oliver?"

Uneasiness slid through her at the question. "Actually, I came by to see him."

"You came by?" The woman pounced on this bit of information. "Are you here now?"

Hearing the woman's urgency, Sammi realized she'd made a huge mistake. She'd assumed the lack of publicity surrounding Oliver's private life meant he had no girlfriend. But here was a woman with Oliver's phone, so obviously he was already in a relationship. Heat flared in Sammi's cheeks as she remembered how she'd blatantly offered herself to him. The power she'd enjoyed in that moment had faded by the following morning.

"I'm sorry," Sammi murmured. "I have to go."

"Wait."

Ignoring the woman's command, Sammi hung up the phone. It instantly lit up with Oliver's number again. Sammi stared at the screen for a long moment, letting the call roll to voice mail. She'd really screwed up.

Despite the voice in her head warning her to leave, Sammi lingered in front of Oliver's building. The need to tell Oliver that she was pregnant hadn't vanished just because he was involved with someone. Sammi had a hole in her life where her own father belonged. She'd never understood why her mother kept his identity from her. How could Sammi live with herself if she did that to her own child? Decision made, she squared her shoulders and lifted her phone.

"Excuse me." The familiar voice jolted Sammi out of her thoughts. A woman had pushed through the entrance to Oliver's building and was advancing on her. "Are you the one looking for Oliver?"

"Um. Well." Cupping a protective hand over her lower abdomen, Sammi backed away from the woman's aggressive approach. "That is…"

"Are you Suzi?" The woman showed every intention of getting answers out of her.

"I'm Sammi." She took another step back, retreating from the woman's determined expression and focused pursuit. This was so much worse than she'd imagined. She extended Oliver's business card. "We met a few weeks ago. He gave me this."

"Sammi?" The woman frowned. "Not Suzi? But you're a model, right?"

"Yes."

"Watch out!" The shout came from behind her and to her right, followed by honking.

Movement caught in her peripheral vision. Something bright red was coming at her fast. So many things registered at once. The horror on the doorman's face. The screech of brakes. And then something was hitting her left side with enough impact to send her flying. Pain exploded in her wrist and shoulder as she landed hard on the sidewalk. Lights flashed in her head, and then all went dark.

Three

In the week since the news had come out that his father was alive and being extradited from the Caribbean, Oliver had taken to leaving his smartphone behind while he roamed Manhattan in search of inspiration. The barrage of calls and texts from his mother and brothers regarding the legal matters surrounding Vernon Lowell left no room for Oliver to think about anything else. Only when he stepped away from the electronic device could he control his focus and direct his attention where he wanted it to go. Unfortunately, the outings rarely lasted longer than a couple of hours.

Putting away his camera, Oliver raised his hand and hailed a taxi. Giving the driver the address of his SoHo loft, Oliver settled back and opened the floodgates to the myriad of his responsibilities awaiting him. Besides the family crisis that dominated his to-do list, he had a business to run and clients that expected results. The strong desire to chuck it all and find his own tropical island to hole up on brought his father to the forefront of his mind. He hated acknowledging this common ground between them, but the similarities were too obvious to ignore.

In rehab, he'd confronted that his drug habit had been all about running away from his problems and learned that only when he faced his demons could he take control of his actions and turn his life around. The stronger he'd become, the more he'd regretted his youthful choices, recognizing if he'd pursued his passion for photography from the beginning instead of trying to please his father by pursuing a business degree at Harvard, he might not have fallen into addiction. Those dark, hopeless years, followed by the harrowing fight to get sober, left him with invisible but painful scars. Yet he couldn't deny that the struggle had not only made him stronger but also allowed him to appreciate his successes.

"Looks like there's something going on at your building," the cabbie said, rousing Oliver from his thoughts.

He leaned forward and gazed through the windshield, spotting the flashing lights of an ambulance up ahead. With the traffic snarled by the emergency, Oliver decided he would get to his destination faster if he walked. After glancing at the meter, he pulled out his billfold and said, "You can drop me off here."

He slid out of the taxi, attention on the pair of EMTs as they loaded someone into the ambulance. Between the numerous bystanders and his approach angle, Oliver couldn't see much detail and wondered what had happened. As his ground-eating strides carried him toward his building's entrance, he spotted a familiar figure in the crowd and made his way toward her.

"What's going on?" he asked, stopping beside his assistant, his gaze on the ambulance as the EMTs slammed the rear doors. Heidi started at his question and turned worried brown eyes his way.

"That woman you asked me to find came by to see you and was struck by a bicycle messenger who swerved to avoid a car that unexpectedly cut him off."

"Suzi?" Oliver's gaze slashed toward the departing ambulance as it pulled away from the curb, stunned that she'd slipped through his fingers a second time. "Did you speak to her?"

"Her name isn't Suzi," Heidi explained, extending his phone toward him. "She called herself Sammi." Heidi held up a backpack. "This is hers. I looked inside, and her name is Samantha Guzman."

Oliver took the bag and his cell phone from Heidi, irritation flaring at his mistake. If he'd only cut short today's outing, he might have arrived in time to save her. "How badly was she hurt?

"She hit her head when she fell and blacked out. That's why we called the ambulance. She came to as the EMTs checked her out and complained that her wrist hurt, but she's really groggy."

Oliver flagged down a taxi and followed the ambulance to the hospital. With Sammi's bag in his hands, he was able to convince the staff that they were together and followed a nurse's directions toward a curtained area where she'd been parked. A hard knot of worry began to unravel at his first glimpse of Sammi—Samantha Guzman—after nearly six weeks, but seeing her lying so still and pale on the gurney tempered his relief.

Her lashes fluttered as he stood just inside the curtain, momentarily rooted to the spot. His breath lodged in his chest as she blinked several times, then gazed around in confusion. He could claim that they had unfinished business or that the amazing sex accounted for his obsessiveness, but the truth was she'd somehow wormed her way past his guards. For six weeks he'd been searching for this woman, and now that he'd found her, Oliver had no idea what to say first. Before he figured it out, a nurse entered the room.

"I understand you were in an accident," she said to Sammi, glancing Oliver's way as she bustled about checking vitals and asking standard questions. "The doctor should be in to check on you in a few minutes. Is there anything else we need to know?"

While the nurse had been busy, Sammi had spied Oliver looming off to one side of the cramped space. Her shock had registered as a brief widening of her eyes before she'd glanced away and not looked his way again.

Now, however, as she hesitated before answering the nurse's question, her gaze darted his way once more. She murmured something too low for Oliver to catch, but he could see her eyes were dark with worry in her white face.

"How far along are you?" the nurse asked, making a note.

"About six weeks."

This time Oliver picked up on her words. *Six weeks.*

That described how long it had been since he'd last set eyes on her. Oliver's heart gave a strange lurch as several things collided in his brain. They'd slept together six weeks ago. She'd appeared at his apartment today. Had she come by to declare that she was pregnant and he was the father? Then he remembered the boyfriend who'd broken up with her the night they met. Wasn't it more likely that he, not Oliver, was the child's father?

At least he hoped that was the case. The idea that Oliver could be a good father was completely outside the realm of possibility. What did he know about being a loving, supportive parent? Absolutely nothing.

The nurse left while he'd been lost in thought, and he missed the chance to flee. Alone with Sammi, he fought for calm.

"You're pregnant?"

"Yes."

Is it mine?

"Is that why you came by today?" he asked, crossing his arms over his chest as his heart thundered painfully against his ribs.

"I thought you should know," she said.

"You thought I should know," he repeated, thoughts racing. "Because you think it's mine?"

She appeared unperturbed by his question. "I know it is."

Although she didn't come right out and tell him he was a jerk for questioning her, he flinched as if she'd flung criticism at him. Oliver frowned.

"I don't know anything about being a father," he said, speaking more to himself than to her.

"And I don't know anything about being a mother." Tears filled her eyes. "I guess neither one of us is ready to be a parent." She lifted her hand to wipe away the moisture trickling down her cheek, then cried out and clutched at her injured wrist.

"Are you okay?" Oliver asked, stepping forward, unsure how to take away her pain.

"I'm sorry." She shook her head. "I'm sure this has all been a lot to take in. I don't expect anything from you. You can be as involved as you wish, or I'll disappear out of your life. I just thought you deserve to know so you could make a decision."

It stung that she'd presumed he was the sort of man who fails to step up and take responsibility. Yet could he blame her? He sure wasn't acting like someone she could count on. What was wrong with him? He'd searched all over New

York for her. Now that he'd found her and discovered that things between them were more complicated than he'd anticipated, all he wanted to do was flee.

Fresh tears poured from her eyes. "Damn. I'm a mess."

Most women looked terrible when they cried, but Sammi's misery only enhanced her fragility and awakened his desire to protect her. Before Oliver could assure her that she was perfectly within her rights to feel upset over her circumstances, a tall man clad in a white coat bearing the hospital's logo entered the room.

"Good afternoon, Ms. Guzman." The doctor gave her a comforting smile. "I understand you've taken quite a fall."

Oliver stepped back, offering Sammi some privacy. Her gaze flicked his way, and he glimpsed anxiety in her eyes. No doubt she'd expect him to bolt. It was the perfect opportunity for him to run off, leaving her to cope with the situation all on her own. Did he really need a whole new set of responsibilities? Wasn't there enough chaos in his personal life with his father's reappearance?

Anger flared as thoughts of Vernon Lowell consumed him once more. Deciding what he needed was some fresh air to clear his mind, Oliver headed for the exit. Ten minutes later, back under control, he returned to the curtained area where Sammi had been and discovered she was gone. His first reaction was panic. Had he lost her again so soon? The backpack in his hands calmed him. He had her information in his grasp.

And as he went in search of a nurse who could explain where she'd been taken, Oliver realized that whether or not she was pregnant with his child, he didn't intend to let her escape until he was ready to let her go.

Sammi wasn't surprised when Oliver slipped out after the doctor arrived. After all, she'd given him permission to leave the entire situation in her hands. Therefore, she was quite surprised when, after a round of tests, including an MRI and a wrist X-ray, she was wheeled into a private room and he was waiting for her.

"I thought you'd gone," she said, relief overwhelming her. She reined in her wayward emotions and concentrated on evening out her breathing. She couldn't presume he'd stuck around because he cared about her even a little. They'd slept together once.

"I just stepped out to give you some privacy, and while I was gone, they took you away for testing." He set her backpack on the rolling table beside her. "How are you feeling?"

She noticing that although his gaze had only briefly touched on her midsection, he didn't ask about the baby. No doubt it would be easier on him if the accident had caused her to miscarry. Sammi shook off the uncharitable thought, reminding herself that he hadn't taken the opportunity to bolt.

"My head hurts, and I'm nauseated," she explained, "but they said that's normal for someone who has a concussion."

"They want to keep you overnight," he said, his gaze flicking toward the doorway, as if he wished he could use it. "Is there someone I should call and let them know where you are?"

Celeste popped into Sammi's mind, but she immediately shook her head. She wasn't done being angry with her mother for suggesting Sammi terminate her pregnancy. "There's no one."

A frown puckered Oliver's brow, indicating he didn't believe her, but Sammi kept her expression resolute. It wasn't as if she could count on her mother to rush over and smother her with concern.

"You need someone to keep an eye on you for the next

couple days," he said, his tone matter-of-fact. "Concussions are nothing to take lightly."

Sammi recalled the argument between her and Celeste. If she intended to follow through on her intention to quit modeling and move into a less expensive apartment, soon enough she'd be on her own.

"I'll be fine." She was proud of her confidence, even as she dreaded the battle that awaited her at home.

Oliver shook his head. "I don't accept that."

Even as she bristled at his bossy attitude, a knot unraveled inside her chest. For a brief moment she leaned into the feeling. What would it be like to have someone take care of her for a change? Someone who liberated her from all her worries and woes. Who lifted the burden of responsibility from her shoulders?

Feeling her resolve weaken, Sammi shook away the tempting thoughts. Her fingers crept over her abdomen and the lifelong responsibility that grew inside her. Despite the doubts about motherhood that she'd shared with Oliver earlier, Sammi was ready for the challenge.

"I don't think you have a choice but to accept it," she said, struggling to stay strong while her head pounded and her muscles screamed protests at her slightest move.

"Why are you being so difficult when all I want to do is make sure you're okay?" he countered, sounding put out.

His concern sent electricity jolting through her. The energy blast momentarily vanquished her aches and pains.

"I'm not being difficult."

Oliver crossed powerful arms over his chest and glared. "I disagree."

"You're not asking me what I need," she said, "but telling me what you think I should do. And I already have enough people in my life doing that."

They glared at each other for several seconds before Oliver blew out a breath and moved to stand beside the bed. His tone gentled as he said, "You came to me, remember?"

"And if I hadn't, we never would've met again." There was the crux of her fear. Not once over the last six weeks had he reached out to her. If she'd never become pregnant and gone to his apartment, she never would've seen him again.

"I had your name wrong. The bar was so loud. I thought you said Suzi. You knew who I was, and I never made an effort to get your full name."

His closed expression left her wondering if the lapse had been intentional. After all, she knew a bunch of models he'd hooked up with in the past. Maybe she'd just been the latest in a long line of one-night-stands.

"Why did you run off without waking me that morning?" he continued.

"I don't have a good answer."

She wasn't about to tell him that she'd dreaded facing an awkward morning-after good-bye.

He reached out and dragged a chair over, settling into it without releasing her from the fierce grip of his gaze. "How about you give me a mediocre answer then."

She raised her right hand and fluttered it as if waving away his question. "What happened between us…" Her cheeks burned. "I was embarrassed."

"Because we slept together?"

"I don't make a habit of going home with men I've just met.

"We weren't exactly strangers." A speculative light sparked in his blue eyes. "You said we'd worked together once."

"You didn't remember me."

"I don't remember much about those days," he admitted. "So that explains why you left the next morning. Why did you stay the night?"

She bit down on her tongue to stop herself from admitting that she'd once had a huge crush on him. Nor did she want to explain that she hadn't wanted to go home and deal with her mother.

"I thought you were into me, and I was definitely into you."

"I was." He shifted backward in his chair, unmoved by her conciliatory half smile. "It wasn't a line when I said I found you fascinating."

Sammi considered him for a long moment before venturing, "But now I'm pregnant."

"You are." His neutral expression made her shiver.

"And that is a complication you'd probably rather avoid."

"Don't assume anything about me."

"I'm sorry." The apology leaped to her lips automatically. She stared out the window, avoiding his stern gaze. "Between the pregnancy hormones and everything that's been happening, I'm feeling overwhelmed."

"Do you want to talk about it?"

Her lips quivered as she tried for a brave smile. "I think the last time we were together I might've mentioned I was looking at a career change. Well, that's going to happen a lot faster now that I'm pregnant."

"What are planning to do?"

"I know I have to move out of my apartment." She dabbed at fresh tears as she recalled her mother's dismay. "I can't really afford it if I'm not working."

"Do you have somewhere to go?"

"Not at the moment. I need to give notice, so I have thirty days to figure it out."

"Do you have someone who can help you? What about your parents?"

"There's only my mom. She's my manager and doesn't want me to stop modeling. We had a huge fight about it before I came looking for you."

"What about your dad?"

"I have no idea who he is." She blamed her concussion for that revelation. "My mom was pregnant with me when she emigrated from the Philippines and never talks about him." Weariness rolled over her. "Dammit." Fresh tears formed and rolled down her cheeks. "I'm not usually like this."

"You've been through a lot today." He offered her a box of tissues. "What can I do to help?"

As much as she wanted Oliver to be someone she could count on, Sammi knew that wasn't realistic. Once upon a time his drug habit had landed him in rehab, or so went the gossip after he'd quit modeling. And although rumors indicated that he'd been sober ever since, it was a well-known fact that, between his exacting demands and short fuse, he was a difficult photographer to work with. She doubted the man was any easier to know.

"Nothing," she said, recognizing that she had to do this on her own. "I appreciate your offer, but I'll be okay."

"I don't doubt that." He paused while she blew her nose, interrupting him. "But at the moment you're in the hospital under observation."

"It's nothing serious," she said, her thoughts focusing on the tiny life beating inside her. "The doctor just wants to observe me for a few hours. I'll be out of here in no time. You really don't have to stick around."

"Stop trying to get rid of me."

Her resolve weakened as he lowered his hand over hers and squeezed. At the gentle contact, her body lit up like a Broadway marquee. Longing surged through her, forcing Sammi to fight the impulse to grab his shirt and draw him close. Her pounding headache and sore muscles faded from her awareness. She could only stare at his soft lips and remember how she'd been swept away by his demanding kisses. A new ache began inside her that had nothing to do with the spill she'd taken. She wanted this man so badly it stole her breath.

"You don't need to worry about me," she insisted weakly, shifting her hand away before she said or did something to betray herself.

"I'm afraid it's a little too late for that."

Four

The sky brightened outside the hospital room window from indigo to lavender as Oliver sat beside Sammi and watched over her dozing form. Although the only obvious damage caused by her fall was her wrapped wrist, her skin's ashen tone worried him. In the six weeks since he'd last seen her, Sammi had gone from vibrant to fragile. He'd photographed numerous pregnant celebrities and they'd all glowed with good health and joy. In contrast, Sammi looked as if she'd been stretched to the point of breaking by exhaustion and stress. Her pale listlessness alarmed him. Regardless of whether she was carrying his child, he found his concern for her on the rise. From the first moment he'd set eyes on her, she engaged his interest. Nothing had happened since to change that.

But with his father's reappearance and the turmoil his trial and likely conviction would cause over the next several months, was this really a good time for Oliver to allow himself to be distracted by someone whose life was equally messed up? He didn't even know if the baby was his. The situation could get ugly if he inserted himself into her life and then the ex-boyfriend reentered the picture.

On the other hand, if he was the father, with his family history Oliver was certain to be a terrible parent. Work kept him traveling a large chunk of the year. No doubt the absences would screw up his kid, and he'd come to resent Oliver the same way Oliver had resented Vernon. The cycle of neglect was doomed to be repeated.

Was he really going to be *that* guy? The one who bailed when things got hard? Why not? Thanks to his father, Oliver had been running from meaningful relationships all his life. From his earliest childhood, rejection was the kiss of death. Every time he'd tried to connect with his father and been dismissed, Oliver had withdrawn behind sneers and acted out to demonstrate his contempt. Yet isolating himself brought no happiness.

Oliver glanced toward Sammi and realized her eyes were opened and fixed on his face. Lightning shot through him at the mixture of joy and relief he glimpsed in the depths of her dark brown eyes. She glanced away, but that didn't stop his heart from pounding.

Maybe it was time for a change.

"You're still here," she murmured, glancing at the clock on the wall. "I've been here all night?"

"The doctor wanted to keep you under observation. You can leave as soon as you feel able."

"I'd really like to go as soon as possible."

"I have a car standing by to take you home."

"You really don't—"

"Need to help," he interrupted, nodding. "So you've said, but I feel responsible for you."

An hour later, the doctor checked her over and she was discharged. Ignoring her continued protests, Oliver wheeled her through the hospital and the glass doors at the entrance to where a black town car sat waiting at the curb.

"Where to?" the driver asked after he'd settled behind the wheel.

Oliver peered at Sammi's profile and marveled at the way his perspective had been transformed. Twenty-four hours earlier, he'd been a self-absorbed bachelor obsessing about the past and the drama surrounding his family. He never imagined that reconnecting with Sammi would present him with a whole new set of challenges or that he'd be looking forward to what the future had in store.

"I think he wants to know your address," Oliver prompted.

Sammi gripped her backpack tightly and stared ahead for several long seconds as if grappling with exposing her private information to him. Oliver waited her out with barely restrained impatience, pondering all he learned about her today and anticipating how much more waited to be discovered. At long last, she gave an elaborate sigh and offered up her address.

When the car stopped at the curb in front of her apartment building, Oliver saw Sammi set her hand on the door handle and caught her arm to forestall her. She shot him a confused look while the driver came around to open her door.

"I'm going to escort you all the way to your door," he explained.

"You don't need to," she said. "I'll be fine."

Oliver shook his head. "Maybe eventually, but not at the moment."

She opened her mouth as if to argue, but no protest emerged. Oliver noted her stiff posture and wondered if it was because of her bruises or her unhappiness with his insistence on aiding her. A moment later he got his answer as she slid away from him toward the open door, wincing as she pivoted on the seat and set one foot onto the sidewalk.

Although she displayed a great deal of fortitude during the walk toward the building, she wavered once they entered the lobby. Oliver offered her his arm, and she sighed as she took it. They made their way toward the elevator in silence. When the doors opened, she tried to wave him off, but Oliver shook his head. He'd promised to deliver her safely to her apartment, and that's what he was going to do. They rode in silence to the tenth floor while he kept a close watch on her pale features and she acted as if he didn't exist. Once they arrived at her floor, she refused his help and made her way down the hall toward her apartment.

"Thank you," she said, unlocking the door and opening it just wide enough for her slim body to slide through. Once she was inside, she turned to face him. "I'm home."

Seeing that she intended to leave him stranded in the hall, Oliver set his hand on the door above her head and regarded her with raised eyebrows. "The doctor said someone should stay with you for the next forty-eight hours. So, I'm not going anywhere until I know you're going to be completely okay."

"I'm going to be fine," she promised, looking vexed that she lacked the strength to shut the door in his face. "You don't need to stay."

He leaned forward and snagged her gaze. "Oh, but I do."

"Seriously, I'm fine."

She held firm for several seconds until a strident female voice came at them like an attacking cat from deeper in the apartment.

"Well, it's about time you got home. Where the hell have you been?"

Sammi's eyes widened in alarm as she glanced back over her shoulder. An older, shorter version of Sammi had appeared. The woman was borderline gaunt in a sleeveless zebra turtleneck paired with black trousers and ankle boots. She was dressed like a trendy twentysomething despite being in her midforties. Oliver guessed this was Sammi's mother.

"You missed the Potts shoot yesterday afternoon," the woman continued with unrelenting censure. "And your agency is screaming mad."

Even though it was barely noon, the woman held a crystal tumbler and looked decidedly unsteady as she marched toward them. Sammi rested her shoulder against the door, visibly shrinking from the incensed woman. Oliver set his palm on her lower back to steady her and felt the shudder that passed through Sammi's slender frame as the woman drew near.

"If you keep behaving like this, they'll fire you, and then where will we be?" Catching sight of Oliver, she narrowed her eyes and gave him a skeptical once-over. Taking in his worn leather jacket, T-shirt and jeans, she sneered. "Who the hell is this?"

"I'm Oliver," he stated coolly, not bothering to hide his disgust at the woman's condition. Although he'd already guessed her identity, he countered, "And you are...?"

His discourteous tone made Sammi gasp, but the older woman was either too inebriated to notice his rudeness or too self-involved to recognize that it was her offensive treatment of her daughter that had irritated him.

"This is Celeste," Sammi introduced, her gaze shifting back and forth like a wary mouse caught between two predators.

"I'm Samantha's mother." Celeste stared daggers at Sammi. "I suppose *this* is who you've been spending time with instead of working? I can't believe you dumped Ty to take up with him."

Couldn't the woman see how fragile Sammi was? Oliver rocked onto his toes, but the urge to shove the abusive woman out of the way and propel Sammi into the apartment dimmed at her stricken look. Although she'd mentioned an argument with her mother, this unhealthy family dynamic was more extreme than he'd expected. And from Sammi's tension, Oliver could see how much it pained her.

Questions bombarded him. Why hadn't she separated herself from this noxious environment? Obviously, her mother didn't have Sammi's best interest at heart.

Celeste's voice shifted from accusation to woe as she added, "Why are you so determined to punish me?"

"She's been in the hospital." Oliver ground out the words, his anger barely suppressed.

He expected the news would provoke a dramatic change in the woman's behavior, but her next reaction he didn't see coming.

"Oh, thank heavens," she said, displaying yet another quicksilver change in mood. "I was worried you wouldn't do the right thing and take care of it. Now you can keep working."

Celeste's obvious delight was a crushing blow, and both Sammi and Oliver stiffened at her mother's shocking insensitivity. That Celeste believed she knew what was best for Sammi without asking her daughter's opinion knocked the breath from Oliver's lungs. He glanced over at Sammi, concern escalating as the blood drained from her already pale face. She looked devastated and utterly defeated. Oliver's temper flared at Celeste's lack of concern for her pregnant daughter's well-being.

"She was in an accident," he declared, charging into the fray like a white knight to defend a damsel in distress. It wasn't a role that he had much experience with, but Sammi seemed incapable of standing up for herself.

"She was knocked down by a bike messenger and has a concussion." Oliver was on the verge of sweeping Sammi into his arms and blowing past her mother when Sammi slapped her hand over her mouth and raced toward a door on the far side of the room.

"Where are you going?" her mother shouted after her, before turning to glare at Oliver. "I suppose you're the father." Celeste took two steps toward him, her hips swaying in her manner that suggested she was the dominant figure in the room. Her scathing assessment dismissed him as a nobody even before she spoke. "You don't look like much. If you think that my daughter is your ticket to better things, you're wrong."

Said the woman who was day drinking and berating her daughter for not working hard enough. Oliver shook his head in disgust. If Celeste was managing Sammi, no doubt she was relying on her daughter's modeling as her source of income.

"You have no idea what you're talking about," Oliver said before dismissing the woman as not worth his time. Pushing past Celeste, Oliver followed Sammi and found himself in a small bedroom. An open door led to an adjoining bathroom where Sammi was splashing water on her face.

"Does she live here with you?"

"Yes," Sammi said, the word muffled as she blotted her face with a towel. "I told you I didn't need your help."

"She's not help. There's no way she's capable of taking care of you."

"She's not usually like this. It's just that I didn't call, so she's been worried."

"She's drunk."

Oliver had no problem slamming Sammi's mother for overindulging so early in the day. He recognized someone with addiction issues, and his gut knotted at the thought of Sammi raising a child in such a toxic environment.

"I don't have a choice." Sammi turned around and leaned back against the sink. "I have nowhere else to go."

"Come home with me. I can promise you quiet and privacy while we sort through everything that's going on."

Her breath hitched, and she knuckled her eyes like a tired toddler. "I can't. I have to stay here."

"You don't *have* to do anything except take care of yourself and the baby. That's all that matters right now." Seeing her exhaustion, he wondered if she realized how much the vivid despair on her face exposed about her feelings regarding her current situation. "Pack a bag and let's go."

Oliver ushered Sammi into a guest room in his spacious SoHo loft and set her overnight bag on the bed. As in the rest of the apartment, the walls had been painted a soft gray. Floor-to-ceiling white drapes framed tall windows and the narrow desk that sat below them. A queen-size bed sat atop a steel-blue area rug whose color matched the throw pillows and blanket draped across the white comforter.

Sammi immediately felt at home in the restful room. "I promise, I won't overstay my welcome," she said, setting her hand on her overnight bag.

"Stay as long as you need to."

"I don't want to intrude."

"Did you look over the recommended list of obstetricians I gave you earlier?" he asked, ignoring her ongoing resistance to his help.

"Not yet."

Although the doctor at the hospital hadn't seen any indication that the fall had affected her pregnancy, he'd recommended that she make an appointment with her obstetrician as soon as possible to have an ultrasound. Since Sammi hadn't yet chosen a doctor, while she'd slept, Oliver had taken it upon himself to locate the best ones in Manhattan.

"Let me know the details when you make the appointment."

His words sent a strong jolt of uncertainty through Sammi. "What for?"

"I intend to go with you."

His determination caused her pulse to jump. She fanned her fingers over her still-flat belly, unsure what to make of his startling change of heart. Part of her wanted to read too much into his support, but so much had happened in the last twenty-four hours… Dare she trust that he'd stick around once this current crisis was over and he realized that being a parent was forever?

"Yesterday you weren't sure this was your baby."

"I'm still not."

"So why are you insisting on being with me for my appointment?"

"I feel responsible. Your accident happened in front of my building." A muscle jumped in his jaw. "Plus, you don't seem the type to make up something that would be easy to disprove."

"You don't know me well enough to say that," she declared, unaccountably frustrated that he trusted her.

"I don't," he agreed. "But the fact that you're trying so hard to avoid my help gives me reason to believe that you believe the baby is mine."

"You realize I could be a master manipulator." Yet even as she said this, she noted his wry expression. Obviously, he wasn't taking her warning seriously. Was she really that transparent? Given the mocking quirk of his eyebrow, she guessed she was. "Okay, fine. Maybe I'm not, but that doesn't mean you shouldn't be wary of me."

If anything, his amusement deepened. "I'll keep that in mind."

What was wrong with her? Why couldn't she just accept his help until she figured out her situation? Heaven knew she had more than enough to worry about between dealing with her mother, remaking her career and finding a new apartment she could afford.

"I have work to do in my studio," he said. "Why don't you settle in and then rest. We can talk over dinner. If you get hungry in the meantime, my housekeeper will fix you whatever you want. Her name is Marie."

"Thank you."

Other words wanted to pour out of her. She had questions about why he was helping her and how he saw the future playing out for them. That he'd led her to a guest room rather than the master bedroom was a good indication that there'd be no more drugging kisses and passion-filled nights ahead of her. She'd have to be content with the memory of his lips trailing over her skin and the way she'd lost her mind as their bodies came together.

"No need for thanks." If he had any inclination where her thoughts had gone, he gave no indication. "I'll see you later."

As Oliver's footsteps retreated down the hall, Sammi's knees buckled and she dropped onto the bed. Had coming here been the right decision? Ever since their first night together, she'd recognized that anything beyond a single night in his bed would end badly for her. His reputation as a hard-partying player who abused drugs and alcohol might be behind him, but he didn't strike her as a good bet for long-term involvement. Yet here she was, ensconced in his SoHo apartment, hiding from her mother, out of touch with reality, unsure of what life-altering issue to tackle first.

The contents of her overnight bag awaited her attention.

She had no idea what she'd packed. Earlier, with Oliver looming in her bedroom doorway, overseeing her efforts as if expecting her to collapse at any second, she'd been too distracted to think straight. Sammi unzipped her bag and began to pull out the things she'd brought with her, forcing herself to make peace with her decision to come here and take stock of what she had to work with. For months now, she'd been wanting a fresh start but couldn't find the breathing room to clear her head and make a plan. Oliver had offered her the peace and space to do so. She would've been a fool not to take it.

Once everything was put away, she settled at the desk with a blank notebook and a batch of colorful pens. Working through her problems was easier when she put pen to paper and made lists. With her thoughts spinning, she wrote *Wants* at the top of the first page and began brainstorming.

At the top of the list was her baby. She hadn't realized how keenly she longed for the child until she registered the concerned expression on the nurse's face after discovering Sammi was pregnant. At that moment, as she'd contemplated whether or not the baby had survived her fall, she'd embraced motherhood with a fervent grip and swore she'd never let go.

Sammi went on to fill the page with her heart's desires, not pausing to edit as she wrote. Not everything was achievable or even all that specific, but the act of emptying herself would open up space for all the actions she needed to take.

Turning the page, she created a to-do list. First of all, she needed to have a conversation with her modeling agency. She hadn't yet told them she was pregnant and hoped she could book some pregnancy shoots while she figured out what to do next. Celeste blithely refused to acknowledge that with each passing birthday Sammi grew closer to the end of her career. Celeste's refusal to recognize that her daughter couldn't model forever had made it hard for Sammi to plan for the future. If only she had some idea what direction to take. She'd never been given a moment's peace to think about what she'd love to do, much less figure out something she was good at.

Next, Sammi needed to give notice and find a new apartment, something more affordable. A shiver ran through her as she considered how badly her mother was going to freak when she learned she had to move. Sammi hardened her resolve. If Celeste didn't have the funds to live on her own, then that was her own fault. She'd been drawing a salary as Sammi's manager for years. Meanwhile, she'd done little to contribute to the cost associated with living in Manhattan, leaving her daughter to foot the bills. Sammi recognized that she'd let her mother take advantage, but without Celeste, Sammi would never have become a success.

Sammi turned the page in her notebook and wrote at the top: *Things I Love*. Then she tapped her pen against her chin and pondered. Nothing immediately came to mind. What was wrong with her? How could she not have things she loved? Frustration and annoyance swirled about her, making clear thinking nearly impossible. *Come on.* There had to be something she enjoyed.

Flowers. She liked flowers. Could she do something with flowers?

She liked shopping and clothes. Doing something in the fashion world made sense, considering she'd been in the industry all her life. Sammi pondered the career shift that Oliver had gone through from model to photographer. She made a note to ask him why he'd chosen to step behind a camera and how he'd known he would be successful at it. She could also reach out to models who'd gotten out of the business. Surely their stories could spark ideas for her.

Feeling less overwhelmed, Sammi contacted her landlord and gave her thirty-day notice. Since she'd leased the apartment fully furnished, at least she wouldn't have a lot to move. With this first step she'd unlocked the immobility that had characterized her existence for the last year. Both relief and terror swept through her. She'd set her foot on the path to her future, and there was no going back.

With the last of her energy, she sent her mother a text and explained what she'd done. Then, too spent to face her mother's wrath, she shut off her phone and set it aside. Lying down on the bed, she rested her palms over her abdomen and closed her eyes. She would picture a future with her baby and keep her focus fixed there. In the midst of her visualization, as she held her new baby in her arms, she was surprised when Oliver's handsome face made an appearance. The joyful satisfaction in his blue gaze made her heart jump.

Her eyes flashed open and she blinked rapidly to reorient herself in the unfamiliar room. She sat up and spent several seconds trying to catch her breath. It was so tempting to imagine him as part of her and her baby's future. But was it realistic? She had a hard time picturing Oliver enjoying the noisy chaos that surrounded children.

The lack of a father in her own life had given her plenty of opportunity to imagine the perfect dad. He was the sort who would get down on the floor and play. Who never complained about changing diapers and adored reading bedtime stories. He would attend every school function and volunteer to coach soccer games. His child would never know harsh words or feel neglected. Their home would be filled with love and happy moments.

Little of that sounded like Oliver.

A light knock on her door brought her off the bed. She crossed the room and answered the summons. The familiar brunette standing outside her door was the same one who'd answered Oliver's phone and confronted her on the street. Oliver's girlfriend. Sammi's stomach sank. In the wake of the accident she'd forgotten all about this wrinkle.

"There's nothing going on between Oliver and me," Sammi began, meeting the woman's startled brown eyes as she rushed to excuse what she'd done, even as a jealous lump formed in her stomach. "He's just helping me out for a few days. You don't need to worry about me."

"Okay…" The woman drew out the word uncertainly. She held a tablet clutched against her chest. "I'm Heidi. Oliver's assistant. He told me to check and see if there was anything you need. If you have a specific dietary requirement, I can leave instructions for his housekeeper."

"You're his…assistant?" Sammi grew light-headed with relief. Not only hadn't she done anything wrong when she'd slept with Oliver, but he wasn't already taken. "Not his girlfriend?"

"Oh, no." Heidi's denial was so vehement that if Sammi wasn't already reeling from everything that had happened to her these last few days, she might have laughed out loud. "Although my boyfriend complains that I'm Oliver's work wife."

"You have a boyfriend." The fact that Sammi had felt possessive of Oliver for even the briefest of seconds demonstrated that she made a mistake coming here. "That's nice."

"Almost two years now," Heidi continued with a broad smile. "Anyway, if there's anything you need, just text me. Here's my number." She extended a business card. "Oliver told me to take good care of you. And that's what I intend to do."

Five

Oliver left Sammi to settle into his guest room and headed downstairs to his studio. As he did every time he needed to step away from things that were bothering him, Oliver intended to lose himself inside his creative process. Today, however, as he looked through the photos he'd taken at a shoot earlier in the week, the issues confronting him were not so easy to shake.

Had inviting Sammi to stay been a mistake? He'd never opened up his home like this to a woman he'd slept with. On the other hand, he'd never slipped up and gotten anyone pregnant before. That is, if the child was even his.

While he didn't regret insisting that Sammi leave her mother's toxic presence, the smart move would've been to put her up in a hotel and hire someone to watch over her for a few days. Instead, he'd not just inserted himself into her life, but by bringing her back to his apartment, he'd also drawn her deep into his. If the situation with her went sideways, how could he eject a pregnant woman from his home after he'd offered her his help?

He wasn't her savior or her friend. Chances were the baby wasn't his and she'd be gone out of his life in no time. Until then he just needed to avoid more complex, charged conversations that dug into the dark places in their psyches.

One thing had become quite clear—the benefit of all that was going on was that Sammi and the potential that he was going to be a father had provided a momentary distraction from the drama surrounding his own family. Rage flooded him as his thoughts turned to Vernon. As Oliver pondered becoming a dad, his own father's selfishness and greed took on even greater malevolence. Had Vernon given a second's consideration to the harm his actions would cause his wife and sons before he ran off? Even worse, had Vernon realized the damage and left anyway?

Although Oliver would avoid his father's mistakes, his track record wasn't exactly a glowing representation of stability and good decision making. He could intend to put his child's needs first, but did he have what it took to make anyone happy? Already he was doubting the wisdom of inviting Sammi to stay.

He wasn't convinced he could resist his attraction to her. Or if he should. Time and distance hadn't dimmed his desire, and during the last six weeks their situation had grown way more complicated.

On the other hand, maintaining an emotional distance didn't preclude him from enjoying the physical chemistry between them. He just needed to be clear and up front about his aversion to any sort of emotional commitment. The last thing he wanted to do was lead her on.

Several hours later, unsatisfied by the work he'd accomplished, he headed upstairs to find Sammi seated at the dining room table, a notebook open before her, the lined page filled with colorful sentences. She sat with one foot braced on the chair seat, her shoulders hunched as she wrote. Instead of the jeans and T-shirt she'd arrived in, Sammi had donned a pair of black wide-leg pants and a tan oversize shirt. Her long dark hair fell around her face, obscuring her profile.

Oliver studied her for several seconds, lost in the lightning flash of attraction she inspired. Now that the crisis resulting from her accident was behind them, his strongest desire was to crush her in his arms and kiss her until they were both delirious and panting. If not for the dark circles beneath her eyes, which enhanced her paleness and fragility, he might have swept her up and taken her to his bedroom.

Instead, he sat down at the table across from her, putting the width of the furniture piece between them to thwart his overpowering need to touch her.

"Did you get any rest?"

"It's impossible when my brain is spinning." Her brown eyes were soft with exasperation. "I have so much to do, and to be honest, most of it terrifies me."

Oliver froze. What was she getting at? He wasn't prepared for the air between them to electrify as she glanced at him from beneath her lashes. His inability to read her didn't stop him from imagining how he'd like to slip her out of her shirt and expose her perfect round breasts with their delightful rosy nipples. His body tightened with need as he let his gaze play over her. If she'd dressed in the oversize clothing to hide her body from him, she'd underestimated his imagination.

His thoughts must've shown clearly in his expression, because her cheeks flushed with healthy color. He worked his jaw to hide a smirk, delighted to see she wasn't immune to the chemistry between them.

"What are you working on?" He gestured at the notebook.

"The rest of my life."

She closed the notebook in a rush before he could read any of what she'd written. Although he appreciated her right to privacy, irritation flared at her vague answer. Oliver shut down the emotion. The extent to which she intrigued him was unsettling.

As curious as he was about her plans, he knew if the tables were turned, he'd resist being pushed to share his thoughts, but he couldn't stop himself from asking, "Come to any conclusions?"

"None." She pulled a face. "I'm just making a list of things I like. What's that phrase? Do what you love and the money will follow."

"What do you love?"

To his surprise, she flipped to a page in the notebook and turned it so he could read her writing. "Here's what I have so far, and none of it is going to produce income."

"I see what you mean," he said, pointing to one item. "Morning sunshine on your face is impossible to package and sell."

"I know." She reached out and took the notebook back before he could make more than a cursory pass. "The problem I'm having is that modeling is all I've ever done." She glanced up at him. "After you quit, how did you decide to become a photographer?"

"I…it was something I liked to do when I was a kid."

"So how come you didn't pursue photography first instead of becoming a model?"

Pain exploded in Oliver's chest. "I didn't think I was any damned good at it," he growled, his stark explanation making her wince. He held still, expecting her to counter with a question. Instead, she waited him out, and her attentive listening encouraged him to keep going. "My brother is a fantastic painter, and even though my dad considered being an artist a hobby rather than a vocation, he appreciated Josh's talent. When it came to me, though… 'Photography is something anyone can do.'" Despite not hearing his father's voice for fifteen years, Oliver mimicked Vernon's derisive drawl perfectly.

"But your work is fantastic," Sammi said, gesturing to the wall where he'd mounted some of his favorite magazine covers. "People connect with it because it's so emotional."

"Emotion wasn't something my father had much patience for." A layer of ice formed over Oliver's soul as he thought back to his childhood and the absence of affection from Vernon Lowell. "He was a coldhearted businessman, obsessed with money and what it could buy. The only way he appreciated art was for its intrinsic value rather than its aesthetic."

Sammi nodded her understanding. "My mom has always treated my looks as a commodity. Even now, when people tell me I'm beautiful, I never take it as a compliment."

That she couldn't appreciate just how heartbreakingly gorgeous she was hurt his heart. Flinching from the pain, he frowned. She deserved to be treated so much better. Was that why she'd sat there and let her ex-boyfriend berate her? She didn't believe in her value enough to fight back? The damage her mother had done mirrored the harm that lingered in his own background.

"I made an appointment with an obstetrician," she began, changing the subject. "When I told them about what happened yesterday, they said they could get me in at eleven tomorrow. I know you're busy. If that doesn't work for you, I understand."

"I told you I would be there and I will."

She nodded, her gaze following the random doodles she was drawing. "Before I called them, I did a little research."

"On what?"

"When I came to see you yesterday, I knew this baby was yours, and because of that, I hadn't given any thought to the fact that you might not believe me."

He could see her disappointment but had no intention of reassuring her. "We can run a DNA test after the child is born."

"That's what I thought too." Her gaze met his. "But then I thought how hard it would be on both of us to wait that long. So, I did an internet search and learned the doctor can pull blood from both of us and run a DNA test that way. It will only take a few days to get the results back. It's completely safe and noninvasive for the baby, and best of all, it's ninety-nine percent effective."

She looked so pleased by her discovery that Oliver found his own mood lifting.

"That's great news."

He'd been dreading that agonizing eight-month wait before learning if he was the father of Sammi's baby. Now he had a path to immediate and definitive proof. That she'd chosen not to drag out the question of paternity made it seem as if she truly believed he was the baby's father. Otherwise, she could've let the mystery drag out for the remainder of the pregnancy and use the time to worm her way into his life in the hopes that she could create some lasting connection between them.

Oliver glanced toward Sammi. Seeing that she appeared to be absorbed in her notebook once more, he took the opportunity to study her. Oblivious to his interest, she'd drawn her lower lip between her teeth and was concentrating on filling a blank page with a new list.

While he might not be open to sharing his life with anyone, he was already keen on the idea that Sammi might stick around. And now that he'd thought about it, Oliver realized this idea had sparked long before he'd awakened to find she'd snuck out before dawn. Maybe he was intrigued only because she'd left before he'd fulfilled his promise to photograph her or because their single night together hadn't slaked his hunger.

"Of course, you don't have to be involved if you don't want to," she said, possibly interpreting his long silence as resistance to becoming a father. "I'm fully prepared to raise this baby on my own."

Had she offered him an escape because she questioned his willingness to step up or his worthiness as a father? And could he blame her for the latter, since he was having similar doubts?

"Let's not discuss the future until we have all the facts," he suggested, realizing that, in a very short time, he might very well need to readjust his thinking. Because in a few days he'd know whether or not his whole life would soon undergo a massive change.

Or maybe it already had.

Two days following her first appointment with her new obstetrician, Sammi woke up in her own bed and reflected on why her body ached in the absence of a man she barely knew. After one sleepless night in his guest room, where she'd tossed and turned, fighting the temptation to walk down the hall and crawl into his bed, she'd packed up and returned home. Staying at his place was too risky. Her preoccupation with him went beyond his role as the father of her baby. How far beyond was what worried her. She was like a planet revolving around the sun, caught in his gravitational pull, unable to break free. Lust. Joy. Anxiety. Belonging. He inspired more emotions than she knew how to handle.

Although she'd rarely gone without a boyfriend, she'd

never thrown herself into a passionate physical relationship nor fallen in love. She'd taken a few lovers, but she preferred companionship over romance. Her mother was needy enough without adding a demanding lover to the mix. The type of men she fell in with liked having a beautiful woman on their arm. To them she was an ornament, a status symbol they could show off to their friends.

In exchange, she had someone who took care of her for a while. Of course, it was all a big illusion. In the end, they either grew frustrated with her indifference and found someone new or pushed her for more than she was willing to give, as in the case of Ty.

Oliver was different. From the beginning he'd shown that he was more interested in her substance than the package it came in. While he wasn't indifferent to her beauty, it seemed to be of no value to him. It was exciting to have a whole new chance at discovering what could be. He didn't need her as arm candy. Yet there was no denying that he was interested in her. At least sexually. The chemistry between them couldn't be denied. The question was whether she should resist.

Until she figured it out, she'd decided it was prudent to move out. As tempting as it had been to continue avoiding her mother and enjoy being fussed over by Oliver's housekeeper, she recognized that the longer she relied on Oliver, the harder it would be to take the steps to live independently. She'd never been on her own, and even though it was her mother who relied on Sammi financially, as frustrating as Celeste could be, Sammi valued the companionship she received in return. Which made it sound like Sammi was an adult child, when in truth it was often easier to let her mother get her way than to stand up to her.

Yet somehow, finding out she was pregnant had given Sammi the determination to stand up to her mother. All the decisions ahead of her seemed less daunting now that she was responsible for her child. Despite all the obstacles before her, the possibilities were endless and exciting.

Feeling stronger and more focused than she had in weeks, Sammi hit the gym to assuage her guilty conscience after slacking off. While she was blessed with the metabolism that let her eat pretty much whatever she wanted and maintain her slim figure, sweating through a workout cleared her mind. Maybe her lack of gym time was one reason for her muddled thoughts of late.

She spied her best friend working out with free weights as she entered and made her way past the gym equipment toward Kimberly.

"Well, look what the cat dragged in," the lanky blonde said, her welcoming smile at odds with her scolding tone. "You've been skipping our workouts for two weeks now."

"I haven't been feeling great," Sammi said, bracing herself to deliver the news.

So far she'd told only her mother and Oliver. She had an appointment to tell her agency later that day. Hopefully, they'd keep her on as long as possible. She needed to earn as much money as she could in the weeks before she started showing.

"I'm sorry to hear that." Kimberly paused between sets and eyed her. "You do look pale and thinner. Are you feeling better?"

Sammi stripped off her jacket and picked up a set of five-pound weights. "The nausea comes and goes."

"If it's been going on for two weeks, you should see a doctor."

"I did."

Her friend's blond ponytail swung as she shot Sammi an inquiring look. "And...?"

"I'm pregnant," Sammi said, delivering the news without preamble.

"Please tell me it isn't Ty's."

Kimberly had made no secret her dislike of Sammi's ex-boyfriend. They'd double-dated on several occasions with Kimberly and her documentary-filmmaker fiancé. Sammi wished she'd taken Kimberly's advice and dumped him sooner.

"Ty is not the father."

"You're sure?" Kimberly fixed her friend with worried blue eyes.

"Very. In fact, we never…"

Kimberly's mouth fell open. "You dated him for almost six months and you never slept with him?"

Sammi nodded. "It never felt right with Ty."

In fact, she'd started wondering if there was something seriously wrong with her, since her libido had seemed on permanent vacation. And then along came Oliver and rocked her universe.

"So who is the father?"

"Oliver Lowell."

"The photographer?"

Sammi's stomach clenched at her friend's surprise. Was Kimberly about to issue another dire warning about Sammi's poor relationship choices? To her surprise, the other model showed curiosity rather than disgust.

"Oh, he's hot," Kimberly said, fanning herself. "And I've heard he's great to work with as long as you take direction well. But I didn't think he was doing fashion shoots anymore."

Sammi thought about the twenty-three dollars she'd paid for a portrait session that had never happened. "I didn't meet him at a shoot."

"Then how? You aren't one for clubbing or parties."

"He approached me the night Ty and I broke up."

"Interesting timing." Kimberly's expression shifted from thoughtful to curious. "So you've been dating all this time and haven't said anything?"

"Not exactly." Sammi hoped her friend would think the heat overtaking her cheeks was due to the workout rather than embarrassment. "It was just that one night."

"That's so not like you." Kimberly gave a shrug. "But I suppose that after Ty dumped you, a hookup makes sense."

"It wasn't like that," Sammi said. "I didn't sleep with him because I was upset that things ended with Ty."

"Then why did you?"

Sammi paused before answering, the memory of that night still holding power over her. "He's charismatic and troubled and so sexy. When I'm with him, I can't decide whether to tear his clothes off or run like hell the other way."

Kimberly's eyes glowed with curiosity. "What usually happens?"

"Neither. You know how I am—I just push it all down and pretend nothing bothers me."

"One of these days all that emotion is going to explode out of you, and heaven help the person who gets mowed down by the rush." Kimberly grinned with relish. "So, obviously you're into him. How does he feel about you?"

"I'm not sure. I guess he was looking for me after the night we spent together, but he didn't get my name right."

"Men," Kimberly scoffed, rolling her eyes. "And now? How is he feeling about his impending fatherhood?"

"I can't quite tell. I mean this whole thing has come as a huge shock, and he's not totally convinced the baby's his." Sammi stretched out her shoulders after a series of overhead circles with a weighted ball. "The paternity test results are due sometime today."

"And then he'll know."

"And then he'll know," Sammi echoed, her stomach clenching.

"Any idea how he'll react?"

"Not a one."

"But you're hoping it's the start of something?" Kimberly ventured.

"I'm not sure."

"But you're really into him, right? Wouldn't it be perfect if he felt the same way about you?"

"I don't know. I mean the sex was amazing, but what if that was all it was for him?"

"You won't know if you don't try again, right?"

Sammi nodded. She'd been thinking along the same lines, but what happened if more great sex led nowhere? Already Sammi felt far too emotionally vulnerable thanks to the pregnancy hormones.

"It's just that I had a huge crush on him when I was a teenager, and I'm lusting after him now big-time. What if I get hurt?"

"What if you don't?"

"I think I should take things really slow."

"Or you could take a crazy risk and see where it leads."

"You are always so optimistic," Sammi said, envious of her friend's confidence. "How do you do it?"

"I owe it all to my parents. They brought me up right."

Having met most of Kimberly's family, Sammi understood where her friend was coming from. With the amount of love and support her parents showered on their three kids, it was no wonder each of them were not just happy but also successful in both their private and professional lives.

"And speaking of parents," Kimberly continued, "how is your mother taking all this?"

"Badly. She's counting on me to model. But I don't really want to anymore, and yeah, I'll stick with it as long as I can. I don't know what else to do."

"I might have an idea for you. It's not much right at the moment, but it could turn into something down the road."

Sammi found herself intrigued. She could always count on Kimberly to offer great advice. She approached everything with a cool head and pragmatic attitude. Any suggestions she might have for Sammi's future would be worth listening to.

"I'm all ears."

"Brody is working with this company that is offering online tutorials and advice. They contract with experts to record lessons or workshops that they will then sell online."

"What sort of things are they interested in?"

Kimberly shrugged. "It's pretty open. They are reaching out to artists, models, actresses, musicians, stylists. Brody wants me to do a series on runway walking. I already suggested that you would be perfect for posing. You are brilliant at both editorial and commercial. You could explain the differences of each." Kimberly cocked her head. "And I'll bet you could do a whole series on your life as a child model. Or what it's like to model overseas."

"That sounds interesting," Sammi said, but even as the idea captured her imagination, she wondered if she had all that much to offer.

"So can I tell him you're in?"

"Sure." Nothing ventured, nothing gained. If that was true, wouldn't the same concept apply to her relationship with Oliver? "Why not."

Six

There it was. Proof definitive that he was a father. The stark reality shut down Oliver's brain and sent a tornado ripping through his awareness. He didn't know which emotion to settle on. Panic seemed a good choice, but he pushed it down. It came as no surprise to Oliver that after all his criticism of his father, all the blame he'd heaped on Vernon's head, every bout of self-righteous rage, when faced with actually proving his claim that he would be a better parent, Oliver was terrified that he'd fail.

Yet he was also excited that a child would be part of his life from now on. And that he would be forever connected to Sammi. Even if the sexual relationship he still wanted to pursue with her eventually fizzled out, he was confident they could remain civil for the sake of their child. After all, no matter how much damage Vernon's wandering eye had caused his wife, they'd stayed married to keep the family together.

Surely he and Sammi could make something similar

work. He was already preoccupied with her welfare and liked the idea that she would become a staple in his life. Even before he'd learned that she was pregnant, his determination to find her spoke to how strongly she affected him. His pursuit had been about more than a night of great sex. From the first moment he saw her, she'd captured his interest, and that feeling had only increased during the hours they'd spent together.

And now that he knew the baby was his, he welcomed that she was a permanent fixture in his life. The nature of their relationship might not be crystal clear, but when he contemplated that she might disappear again, he began thinking of ways to bind her to him, her and the baby. The three of them would become a unit. With Sammi and their baby he would achieve the belonging he'd never known as the extra son, the unwelcome third wheel of twins Jacob and Joshua, Vernon Lowell's spare heir, or even his mother's third born.

But what if that wasn't how things played out? What if he let himself need Sammi and she had different ideas about how their relationship should go? It made perfect sense that they would agree to co-parent and coordinate to raise their child together. But she'd already insisted she was ready to raise the baby on her own. Would she resist his vision for them? She'd been raised by a single mother and had her own notion of family. And given the trouble brewing for the Lowell family, would she even want to connect herself and her child with them?

Anger flared as Oliver contemplated how the scandal surrounding Vernon's reappearance was poised to disrupt his life once more. Why couldn't his father have just stayed gone? Instead, the past was going to be dredged up again as if the last fifteen years hadn't happened. Oliver had worked hard to overcome not only his family's ruined reputation after the embezzlement scandal that rocked Black Crescent Hedge Fund but also his own bad behavior in the wake of his father's villainy. The trial would revisit all the evil Vernon had done and keep Oliver and everyone close to him in the news. Sammi and their baby included.

Yet when his doorbell rang and he opened the door to see her standing in the hall, all worry vanished. Sammi squeaked in surprise as he swept her off her feet. His heart bumped as she wrapped her arms around his neck, her soft breath puffing across his cheek.

"Oliver," she protested, soft laughter in her voice. "What are you doing?"

"Carrying the mother of my child anywhere she wants to go," he replied.

"I take it the results appeared on the testing service portal?"

"Yes."

With caution in her eyes, she scrutinized his expression as he carried her into his apartment. "So you're okay?"

Her words struck him square in the diaphragm. His breath hitched. Had he really treated her with such skepticism? Maybe in the beginning he doubted her, but the second she agreed to a paternity test, he should've known that she couldn't possibly be lying.

"I think I started to believe you when you researched the in vitro paternity test," he said, conscious that his reassurance was late in coming. Too late? Had he retreated too far into self-protection and built a wall between them that would be impossible to tear down?

"You did?" Her wariness struck a chord.

"I was wrong not to reassure you."

"I get it." Her sweet smile banished his worries. She bore him no resentment. "You are famous and rich. I imagine all kinds of women would like to be your baby mama."

Although her tone was lighthearted, her eyes remained somber.

"I'm glad that woman is you."

He set her down near the couch, and they stood facing each other. Their gazes locked as the significance of their new reality sank in. They were going to be parents. In a silence so intense that Oliver could swear he heard their heartbeats begin to synchronize, he lifted his hand and caressed her cheek. Without knowing it, they'd been actively moving toward this moment for weeks, yet they were virtual strangers.

"We've got a lot to talk about," Oliver said. "That's why I asked you to meet me here."

"Can we talk over dinner? I'm starving."

"You are eating for two."

"Some days I feel like I'm eating for four. I'm hungry all the time." She made a face. "When I'm not nauseated, that is."

"Four?" The thought of having multiple children with her struck him like a bolt out of the blue. He never imagined having any children, and now he could see his entire life thrown into chaos by the rambunctious, beautiful clutch of children they made together. "Is that how many you want?"

"Oh, no." She sounded so sure that he frowned. "I can assure you I'm only having one."

For no good reason her answer disappointed him. "Big families have their pros and cons," he said, thinking about his childhood and the dynamic of having twin brothers who were five years older. "Did you only ever see yourself with one?"

"To be honest, I never imagined myself with any." This revelation matched how he'd always thought his life would play out and left him wondering how the pair of them were going to cope.

Oliver enfolded her in a friendly hug. "I think you're going to be a great mom."

Instead of boosting her confidence, his compliment seemed to frustrate her. "How can you say that when I don't have any idea what sort of mother I would make?"

"Neither one of us has a great childhood to draw from, so I guess we'll just have to make it up as we go. At least we know what not to do, and I for one intend to put our child's needs first."

"Says every terrible parent ever," she murmured. "What if we're no better?"

When he'd first put his arms around her, Sammi had tensed. Now she set her forehead against his shoulder and let all resistance bleed from her muscles. Her warmth moved into him like rare whiskey, heating his blood, encouraging his hands to wander. He sent his palm coasting along her spine while need built into something intense and unstoppable. Her back arched beneath his caress, bringing her flat belly into light contact with his lower abdomen. The resulting lightning bolt forced him to swallow a groan.

"You don't really believe that." He set his hand beneath her chin and tilted her face up. Her anxiety made him eager to reassure her. "How about we focus on what will make our child happy?"

"And if that means all the toys money can buy?" She arched her eyebrows. "What happens if we spoil our child rotten and end up with a rotten child?"

Oliver widened his eyes in mock horror. "Suddenly I'm terrified."

"Suddenly?" She laughed. "I've been barely holding it together since the first positive pregnancy test."

"The first one?" he echoed, his spirits lifting at her grin. "How many did you take?"

She grimaced.

"We'll just try to do the best we can and balance freedom and boundaries. Play with work. And make sure we show how much we love him or her."

Oliver hadn't grown up knowing a lot of physical affection. The only time he was sure that his brothers loved him was when they let him win at a video game or took a couple of minutes to help with homework or offer pointers on his free throws. And his mom was too busy with keeping up appearances in her social circle to provide any motherly love. Nor had Sammi shown any sign that she was given to unrestrained hugs or spontaneous touching, and he'd guessed her mother was the reason why.

Yet here they stood with their arms locked around each other, committing to being better parents than the ones who'd raised them.

"We can do this," he murmured, his jaw tight with determination.

"Of course we can." Her fervent vow made his heart ache. "And we will."

And then he was threading his fingers through her silky hair and drinking in the spicy floral scent of her perfume. She trembled beneath his gentle touch, whisking him back to those delicious hours with her in his bed, their bodies wrapped together in slick, naked glory. Arousal coursed through him, making him greedy to revisit those long hours. Oliver drew her to him harder than he intended. Desire pooled in his belly as her thighs pressed against his, the contact whipping up a thunderstorm in his emotions.

For days he'd believed that he could treat her like any other woman he desired, enjoying his time with her and then setting her free. Discovery that he was the father of her baby complicated their situation.

Oliver knew he should let her go. But he didn't…couldn't release his grip and set her free. Hunger roared. Need battered him. He cupped her face in his hands and bent down to press his lips to hers. He hadn't planned to kiss her, but as with every other time they touched, his body had a mind of its own.

Before the kiss overheated, the tentative pressure of her hand on his chest shattered the stranglehold of his libido. She turned away from his kiss, her breath coming in ragged pants. Frustration consumed him, the charged emotion coming from a deep-rooted wound.

"I want this," she confessed, ducking her head until her words were almost indistinct. "But I'm not sure I should."

"I get it," he lied, reeling from the sting of disappointment.

Although it felt like one, Sammi hadn't delivered a rejection. She was just demonstrating more restraint than he could summon. She seized her lower lip between her teeth and worried at it. Crushing a groan between his molars, he tore his gaze away and suppressed the memory of her mouth yielding to his. Somehow, he mustered the willpower to take that first, difficult step backward. His chest ached as he moved away from her.

"I mean with everything that's going on…" she continued, trailing off as she noticed his retreat. "It's a lot more complicated now, don't you think?"

"Much more," he agreed, sending his hands plunging into the pockets of his jeans. All too aware of the uncomfortable pressure behind his zipper, he swallowed a curse and changed the topic. "Earlier you said you were hungry." He glanced at his watch. "Let's go have dinner."

The thirty-day notice Sammi had given on her apartment was disappearing faster than she realized. Between long days spent in photo shoots and evenings spent in Oliver's company, she'd delayed finding someplace new to live. She was hampered by the fact that she'd never been in charge of her circumstances before and had no idea how to navigate the New York real estate market, and the person she'd normally turn to for help was the one whom Sammi had hurt the most with her decisions.

Celeste had barely spoken a dozen words to Sammi in the last week, and the silent treatment left her feeling isolated and edgy. She didn't want to fight with her mother. Sammi craved Celeste's approval and support. It seemed so unfair that she'd done everything her mother had ever asked of her, and the moment that she sought to live her own life, Celeste couldn't let go.

Maybe if she'd made some attempt to assert her independence before this. At twenty-six, Sammi recognized that she should've taken responsibility for her finances and made all the decisions about her career, but her mother had always been in charge, and only recently, when Sammi began to contemplate her future endeavors, had the trap of her dependence become clear.

Nor could Sammi bring herself to ask any of her friends for help or advice, fearing that they'd look down on her for failing to act like an adult and take charge of herself. In fact, with her mother's control so firmly in place, Sammi was amazed she'd accomplished as much as she had.

Which was why she'd decided to ask Oliver for help with her apartment search. He'd already seen firsthand what her mother could be like and hadn't judged Sammi's complex bond with a parent who was both selfish and selfless, bully and champion.

Aware how easily she could come to rely on Oliver, Sammi was determined to remain sensible about him, especially in light of all the attention he'd been showering on her. It hadn't been easy. For the past week, he seemed determined to cement himself in her life. He took her to dinner every night and secured the most amazing seats at an off-Broadway show that she'd been dying to see. Sammi tried to make light of his attentiveness, but that was easier said than done. She was living out her fondest teenage fantasies, and each day the fairy tale felt a bit more real.

Yet not everything was rosy. She couldn't help but notice the ever-increasing media frenzy that had begun with the news that Oliver's father was returning to New York to face criminal charges. The first time she'd asked Oliver about it, he'd shut her down hard. Unable to talk to him about it, she'd satisfied some of her curiosity by reading all she could from articles that revisited the old scandal surrounding the disappearance of the money Vernon's friends and clients had invested in the exclusive and wildly successful Black Crescent Hedge Fund.

When the funds vanished and Everett Reardon, Vernon's best friend and Black Crescent's CFO, had been killed in a car crash while trying to elude capture, everyone speculated that Vernon was dead, as well. In the fifteen years that followed, Oliver's older brother Joshua devoted his life to rebuilding Black Crescent and repairing his family's tarnished reputation.

Oliver's phone was buzzing in his pocket. They were in the back of a taxi, on their way to a preview event at a friend's gallery. Sammi sat beside him, hands buried in the pocket of her wool trench coat, her senses buzzing pleasantly at his nearness as he pulled out his phone and glared at the screen. She'd lost count of how many media calls he'd dodged. Peppered with requests for interviews, he made sure their outings took place in quiet venues, overlooked by reporters and paparazzi. He hadn't been keen on publicity before his father's reappearance had focused the spotlight on him. With each day that passed, he was having a harder time avoiding the statement the media was clamoring for.

"I don't know why they're so damned determined to interview me," Oliver groused. "I was in high school when the Black Crescent scandal broke."

Oliver had been only vaguely mentioned in the news articles about the hedge fund, including those from fifteen years ago and the one published a few months earlier that had focused on Joshua as CEO. In addition, Sammi had found only one mention of Black Crescent in any of the stories that focused on Oliver and his photography. Or at least that had been the case until a month earlier, when Vernon had been extradited by the Feds from the Caribbean island where he'd been hiding and flown to New York to face charges.

"It's my father who's newsworthy."

"And you're his son," she reminded him, glad he was sharing his frustration with her instead of letting his anger fester.

"When this whole thing started it was my older brothers who caught the heat. Few news outlets cared about a teenage kid."

Sammi shot him a skeptical look. "Did you forget that your drug addiction was newsworthy? But now you're a world-famous photographer who is as enigmatic as he is brilliant."

"Enigmatic?" He arched his eyebrow, pondering the word. "I would think most people would describe me as difficult or volatile."

"That's your professional side," she countered. "No one knows anything about your personal life. And you work hard to keep it that way. That's why if you are seen around town with the same woman a few times, everyone would assume you're involved with her."

With all the splashy headlines surrounding the upcoming trial for Vernon Lowell, Sammi had wondered how long before her connection with Oliver would surface. Was she ready for her low profile to change overnight?

He snorted. "Is this your way of asking me how many women are rotating through my bed?"

"Ah…no." She cleared her throat. "I mean…" More throat clearing. "It's none of my business who you see."

"Do you think it should be?"

Sammi shook her head. "Of course not. I mean you and I don't have that sort of relationship." Abruptly the car changed lanes, and the momentum pushed her toward him. Her thigh brushed his and made her pulse jerk. Sammi should've shifted away, but snug against his hard body felt so right, so good. "I want us to be… I think we should be friendly. Friends."

A partial truth. Despite her efforts to resist, he held her enthralled.

"And I want to sleep with you again."

"What? You do? We shouldn't." Oh, but she wanted to. So very much. The only thing that had enabled her to hold out this long was knowing that the moment she let herself fall, she wouldn't be able to stop until she was deeply in love with him. Glad for the darkness that hid her eager expression, she bumbled on, "I mean…that could…complicate—" she paused for breath and commanded her racing heart to calm down "—our situation. And neither one of us wants that."

"You're right."

Good. At least they were both on the same page.

His next words shattered that assumption. "But I think it will only get complicated if we let it."

Sammi ejected her breath in frustration. Easy for him to say. He wasn't fighting a crush that went back eight years. "And how do we not let it?"

"We need to be honest with each other." He turned his

upper body in her direction, caught her shoulder and compelled her to face him.

She put her palm on his chest to steady herself against the movement of the taxi and to keep some distance between them. "Honest how?"

"Tell the truth about how we feel. You were right about what you said earlier. I'm very private when it comes to my personal life and don't open up to anyone. But with you I have things that I want to talk about. Things that I haven't told anyone before."

His declaration caused her head to spin. How could she not be swept away by such a flattering admission? Sammi's toes curled in her tall black boots.

"There's more to it than just speaking the truth," she said, unsure she was ready to hear everything he wanted to say. "We'd also have to agree to listen with an open mind. Do you think you could do that?"

"I'm not big on listening," he admitted. "I'm more of a 'boss everybody around until I'm happy' sort of guy."

The car's momentum abruptly changed as the driver was forced to brake. Thrown off balance, Sammi gripped Oliver's thigh, eliciting an inarticulate sound from him. When she peered at his expression from beneath her lashes, his hungry stare made her stomach drop.

"But for you," he murmured. "I'll try."

Emboldened by the possessive light in his eyes, she leaned into his hard body. "Then I guess I should confess something to you." She flattened her breasts against his chest, eliminating the last bit of space between them. "I had a huge crush on you when I was a teenager. So, when you say nice things to me, it feels like I'm seventeen again and completely out of my depth."

Oliver studied her through heavy-lidded eyes. "Are you telling me that sweet talk is the way to your heart?"

Was he really interested in capturing her heart? Would he treat it well once he took possession?

"It's one way," she replied, mustering an inscrutable smile.

"Is there another way?" he asked, lowering his head until his lips hung over hers.

The invitation was hers for the taking. Feeling daring, she lifted her hand and brushed her thumb across his lower lip. He smiled, the expression a sexy, sweet hammer blow to her faltering resistance.

"Later tonight you could take me to Max Brenner," she suggested, naming a well-known chocolate bar near Union Square. "I have a sudden craving for chocolate."

Seven

"This is terrible." Oliver barely restrained a shudder as he stared around the East Harlem two-bedroom apartment.

"It's not terrible," Sammi countered, waving at the west-facing windows. "There's tons of light and the wood floors are beautiful."

"The appliances are old. There's no closet space." He took a step toward the front door. The longer he stayed, the more the dull cream walls seemed like they were closing in on him. "And it's barely eight hundred square feet." Half the size of her current place.

"It's less to furnish." Her voice held a note of forced confidence as she opened the door to the second bedroom, revealing a room that was smaller than his walk-in closet. "I can fit a crib and a changing table in here, no problem."

"It's awful," he declared definitively.

"It's not awful."

They were squabbling like old friends, the exchange heated but without any hostility. During moments like these, Oliver could scarcely believe Sammi had been in his life for only a few weeks. She felt like an old friend from back home that had been with him through the best and worst times.

When reporters pestered him, she refrained from asking questions, offering him empathetic silences that had in turn prompted him to share what he knew about his father's crimes and how that had torn his family apart.

"You can't possibly imagine yourself going from where you live now to this," he said, picturing her Midtown apartment with its high ceilings, spectacular views and stylish furnishings.

She returned to the middle of the empty room and crossed her arms. He kept his face impassive as he took her in. She wore ripped jeans, leopard-print pumps and a fuzzy white sweater that invited him to run his hands all over her. That she wore a stubborn expression kept his libido in check, but the more time he spent with her, the less he understood why he was resisting his attraction for her.

"It's affordable," Sammi persisted. "I made a budget and I intend to stick to it."

"I don't want my child living here." Oliver faced her, mirroring her stubborn defiance, equally determined in his opinion. "Let me find you a nice building with a doorman." He'd considered offering her the house in Falling Brook he'd bought years ago and never used, but he wanted them nearby so he could keep close tabs on both of them.

"That will cost me double what I'd be paying up here."

Oliver ground his teeth at her resistance. This was the fifth apartment she'd brought him to and no more suitable than the last four. "Then let me help."

"No."

She was growing more independent by the day, and

while Oliver cheered her budding self-reliance, he wished she'd listen to reason.

"When I agreed to help with your apartment hunting, I assumed that you asked because you wanted my opinion."

"I do."

"Then take it." He caught her by the elbow and turned her toward the exit. "This is not the place for you."

She made a half-hearted attempt to free herself but in the end allowed him to propel her out the door. No doubt she wasn't as optimistic about the units they'd toured as she wanted him to believe.

"It's been two weeks since I gave my thirty-day notice," she told him, approaching the town car that had been driving them around Manhattan all afternoon. "I'm going to be homeless if I don't find something this week."

While Sammi slid into the back seat, Oliver murmured instructions to the driver, before following her in. As the car started off, he noticed that her earlier energy had washed away. She looked defeated, and he put his arm around her shoulder. The gesture was meant to comfort her, but the delightful softness of the white sweater beneath his fingers made it nearly impossible to avoid petting the fuzzy fabric and the slim arm beneath. With her tucked against his side, the craving to taste her soft lips increased. He pinched the bridge of his nose with his free hand and wrestled with temptation.

He wasn't accustomed to feeling possessive about any woman. The girls he dated in high school blurred into a string of women he could barely remember from the years he'd spent modeling. These days, sobriety hadn't made him any less selfish, but he'd grown more mindful of his actions.

"You aren't going to be homeless," he assured her, his voice gruff with the desire flowing through his veins. "You don't have any furniture to move, just some clothes and personal items, so you could find something temporary while you keep looking."

"I'm trying to save money." She bent over her phone and began tapping the screen. "There's one more place to see. Maybe this one will be better."

"No." Oliver plucked the phone from her hands and held it beyond her reach. "We are not going to look at another apartment in a rat-infested walk-up."

"Oh, please," she countered. "Every one of those buildings was perfectly nice. They just don't happen to be up to your overly inflated standards."

"My standards are perfectly reasonable," he said.

"You grew up in a big house, with a chef, chauffeur and maids to keep everything running smoothly."

"I'm not suggesting we hire you staff." Oliver exhaled in exasperation. "I just want my child to have the best of everything. Is there something so wrong with that?"

"I'll have you know that until I walked my first runway, my mother and I lived in places even smaller and less cared for than what we looked at today."

Oliver winced at the hurt in Sammi's voice, starting to see where he'd gone wrong. "I didn't mean—"

"Those were the happiest days of my childhood, because even though we didn't have much, my mom was always finding ways to have fun for free. Whether it was trips to the library or picnics in Central Park, Thursday evenings at the Children's Museum of the Arts or a ride on the Staten Island Ferry."

As he listened to Sammi recount her fondest childhood memories, Oliver found himself envying her. He thought about the fishing rod his father had sent from the Caribbean two months earlier and how the gesture had been too little, too late. What he wouldn't give to have a collection of father-son experiences he could draw upon when his own child arrived.

"Sounds like she was a great mom and that you two were really close." Yet given the tension he'd witnessed between mother and daughter, he couldn't help but wonder when things had changed. "I don't have any memories like that."

Sammi shot him a sideways glance. "No, I imagine you did the sort of things I couldn't dream of. Like box seats for a Yankees game or helicopter rides around the city. Luxury vacations and backstage passes to the hottest concerts."

"I guess I did some of those things," Oliver said, recalling his friend's birthday party where they'd spent the night at the American Museum of Natural History. "But I honestly don't remember my parents being around for any of them."

"Why were they gone so much?"

"They had a hugely active social life because of the success of the hedge fund my father founded, the one he's in prison for stealing money from. There was always some event or another that kept them from showing up for school events or big games." Oliver made no effort to hide his bitterness.

"I'm sorry," Sammi said, setting her hand on his knee, the innocent gesture making his pulse jump. "I didn't mean to stir up sad times. My mother changed a lot when my career took off. Suddenly I was making more money in a month than she'd make in a year, and it began to consume her."

"So, you're looking at tiny apartments, hoping to re-create your happy childhood, and I'm trying to throw money at you because that's what my parents did in an effort to appease me."

Sammi leaned her head against his shoulder. "Maybe we need to meet somewhere in the middle."

Oliver handed back her phone, contentment humming across his nerve endings, awakening his desire to lose himself in her. "It would be nice if every one of our disagreements ended this well," he said, covering her hand where it rested on his leg. The stirring behind his zipper drowned out sensible thought.

"I don't think you should count on that happening."

"You're planning to cause trouble for me at every turn, aren't you?" He turned his head and grazed his lips over her smooth forehead.

There was a smile in her voice when she answered. "Trouble's in the eye of the beholder, don't you think?"

The car stopped in front of his building before he had a chance to respond. Sammi shifted away from him and glanced out the window. Recognition widened her eyes.

"What are we doing here?"

"Come upstairs and let's talk."

"Talk?" she echoed, a frown appearing. "About what?"

Instead of answering, Oliver opened the door and slid out. Once he stood on the pavement, he turned to find Sammi still sitting in the car. She worried her lower lip between her teeth.

"You don't trust me?" he asked, flooded by bitter resentment. The emotion caught him by surprise. Nothing Sammi had ever done before aroused such a strong negative reaction. This feeling was usually reserved for interactions with his family.

"Of course I trust you. That's not what this is about." With a sigh she took his hand and set her foot on the pavement. "Fine, let's go upstairs and talk."

Thanks to Sammi's show of great reluctance, Oliver felt no satisfaction at convincing her to do as he asked. Instead, irritation kept him from offering reassurance as they entered his building. Then, as the elevator rose to his floor, his increased heart rate caught him by surprise. Although he'd been pondering his decision for several days and thought he was at peace with it, Oliver found himself gripped by anxiety. He hadn't realized until now how important it was for her to say yes to his proposal.

"You asked for my help in finding a place to live," he began, leading her into his living room. "Now you're going to listen to me."

Given the tight set of her mouth, she looked poised to argue. Instead, she merely raised her eyebrows and waited for Oliver to reveal his plan.

"I think you should move in with me."

"What?" She goggled at him. "No. That's crazy…" She paused. "I mean, I couldn't put you out like that."

"You won't be putting me out." He took both her hands in his and let his thumb play over her skin. "You need a place to stay. There's plenty of room here." He wanted to keep her close while her pregnancy advanced. The idea of watching her grow round with his child thrilled him in a way he'd never imagined possible. "And this way, I won't have to worry about you or the baby."

"When you say *move in*…" Her cheeks grew rosy as she assessed his expression. "You mean as roommates, right?"

Her need to clarify the arrangement sent desire through him like a current of electricity. Suddenly every cell in his body was sizzling with awareness. His senses alerted him to the clammy grip of her fingers, the peppermint coolness of her nervous laugh, and the play of relief and regret in her brown eyes.

"I want you to be comfortable," he replied, deliberately keeping his answer vague.

"And what happens if I get so comfortable living with you that I don't want to leave?" A smile ghosted across her lips at whatever she believed his expression had revealed.

"Oh, don't worry. I have no more desire to live with you than you have for me to invade your bachelor space."

"You wouldn't be invading, and it isn't exactly a bachelor space." Frustration flared. He knew she wasn't immune to him, so why did she persist in keeping him at arm's length?

She gave him a wry look. "You are a bachelor. And it is your space." She pulled her hands free and widened the distance between them. "Give me a couple days to think about it, okay?"

"What's there to think about? You want to be practical. I'm offering you a way to save a great deal of money." He was hoping that using logic would up the appeal of his offer. "Think of your budget."

He knew the speed with which her body was changing would soon affect her income. She'd already had to skip casting calls for next spring's New York Fashion Week, and even her hopes of acting as a maternity model had dimmed because so many fashion firms used regular models with fake bumps.

"I haven't been able to think about anything else," she grumbled.

Hearing the surrender in her voice, Oliver relaxed. "Moving in with me is a smart option."

"Is it?" she countered, expelling a hearty sigh. "I took the easy way out and let my mother make decisions for too long. Now I feel like I'm making the same mistake with you."

"I don't want to control you," he said. "In fact, I made the suggestion for purely selfish reasons."

"Such as?"

Letting her long wool coat slide off her shoulders, she cast it onto a nearby chair and took a step toward him. That was all the encouragement he needed to move into her space. She shivered as he gripped her chin and tilted her head so he could study her expression. Hunger tightened in his gut at the longing in her eyes. His heartbeat was a booming gong that sent shock waves reverberating through him.

"I enjoy being with you," he murmured. Consumed by wonder, he sifted his fingers through her silky brown locks. "From the start there's been something between us."

"I feel it too," she whispered. "The apartment search was an excuse to spend time with you."

With a low growl, Oliver pulled her into his arms. As her closeness warmed his whole body, he found sanity slipping from his grasp. Poised as they were on the verge of taking things to the next level, he was wary of pushing too hard, too fast. He slid his palms up her back, the fuzzy sweater slipping evocatively against his skin, and cupped her face. His muscles protested as he held perfectly still and captured her gaze with his.

"Tell me," he urged, his voice roughened with hunger as he let his lips drift from her temple to her ear, "how you want this to go."

"I want…" The rest of her words were lost to a gasp as he brushed the tips of his fingers over her nape.

His eyelids drifted shut, hoping he could hold still until she gave him some sign. The uneven cadence of her breathing mirrored the unsettled thump of his heart as he awaited the rest of her answer. When she shuddered, he realized she was waging her own internal war. This gave him some hope. If they were on the same page on this one thing, surely they could figure out the rest. Her small hand gripped his biceps. Sparks exploded in his mind. His whole body vibrated with anticipation.

And then she whispered, "I want to be with you."

Electricity somersaulted down his spine and sent tingling energy dancing across his skin. He leaned close enough to kiss her and paused while his fingers traced along her jawline to the elegant curve of her neck. He didn't rush. Last time they'd come together in a frantic hurricane of demanding kisses and white-hot caresses. This time he touched her with more care, making her tremble and her chest heave with each fitful breath.

"Oliver." She moaned his name like a plea, and there was only so much strength in his self-control. "Kiss me."

And so he did.

Sammi swayed at the first brush of his lips against hers. The teasing, gentle stroke made her hum. That he intended to take his time with her was clear from the butterfly sweep of kisses across her eyelids and down her nose. Desire shimmered to wakefulness, flashed like lightning and filled her to bursting. She gripped him around the waist and held on as he drew her lower lip into his mouth and gently sucked. Hunger built as his tongue stroked into her mouth. Her blood raged as she clung to him, needing more.

Her lashes fluttered as his strength surrounded her. Wrapping her arms around his neck, she gloried in the erection pressing against her. He was everything she wanted, and she used her lips and hands to tell him so. The world spun around her as he nipped her throat. She moaned in frustration as his hands skimmed over her curves, the barrier of her clothes dulling the sensation of his touch. Even still, his urgency was wildly exciting. She began to writhe against him, tunneling her fingers through his wavy hair and fusing their lips together. His tongue danced with hers, plunging in and out of her mouth, a tantalizing prelude for what was to come.

She was drowning in bliss when he swept her into his arms and carried her down the hall to his bedroom. With her arms wrapped around his neck, he crossed the room in two long strides and stopped beside the bed. And stilled.

Before she knew what was happening, he'd lowered her feet to the floor. A moment later he jerked his hands back and stared down at her. She grasped his arm, her nails flexing into his muscles, protesting his retreat.

As his blazing blue eyes captured her full attention, Sammi realized they hadn't yet reached a point where it was impossible to stop. Had he come to his senses? Were they to remain platonic and avoid heartache?

"Oliver?" Her lungs seized as panic gripped her. He couldn't stop. She needed him. Why didn't he understand that he was everything she wanted? "What's wrong?"

"Sammi…"

His immobility made her heart sink. Had she pushed him away once too often? Of all times for him to listen. Was he going to pick this moment to agree that sleeping together again would be a mistake?

"Damn you, Oliver Lowell," she raged, grabbing his shirt and shaking him as concern etched his handsome features. Need sparked in her stomach, before surging downward. "Don't you dare go all noble on me now."

He was giving her an out. The realization made her furious. Something raw and irrational raced through her. She embraced the recklessness. If he needed her to demonstrate that she wanted him, then she'd do just that. Sammi wrestled with his T-shirt until she succeeded in stripping it over his head. They stared at each other, and the only thing breaking the silence was their panting.

"Don't hold back," she whispered, her cheeks on fire. "Tell me what you want to do to me."

This seemed to be the cue he'd been waiting for, because he slid his hands beneath the hem of her sweater and skimmed it over her head. The air struck her skin and made her shiver. His eyes darkened as they trailed over the nearly transparent material.

"I want to suck on your breasts until you moan," he said, feathering his fingertips over her bra's delicate lace cups.

Hunger tightened her nipples to hard buds and wrenched an inarticulate sound from her throat. She caught a glimpse of an irrepressible smile as he lowered his head and drew his lips along the edge of the fabric, near her skin, but not quite touching. As frustration coiled in her belly, she reached behind her and popped the hook. When the bra loosened, he pinched the fabric between his fingers and pulled it aside, baring her to his gaze.

He licked his lips as if anticipating a tasty treat, and then his mouth was moving over her, dusting kisses over the curve of one breast and then the other, leaving her tight nipples unattended and forlorn. There was none of the promised sucking, but she did moan. And she dug her nails into his head, half-mad with wanting.

"Oliver, what are you waiting for?" She quaked as he blew on her nipple, before rolling the sensitive bud between his thumb and forefinger. "You said you wanted to…suck."

The last word emerged as a strangled cry as he finally drew her nipple into his mouth with firm pressure. This time she wasn't sure what sort of noise she made, but his approval hummed against her skin.

"What else?" she purred, shimmying her hips as he slid her jeans down, leaving her clad in the lacy white panties that matched her bra.

"Hell, babe." He cupped one hand behind her head and one over her mound, applying exquisite pressure as he explored the arousal-dampened fabric. "You are so wet."

"For you." She murmured the words an instant before his lips found hers again.

Meanwhile, his fingers pulsed against her clit, the slow movement making her whimper as the tantalizing caress made her body burn.

"And sweet…" As he nuzzled and nibbled her neck, he kept up the knee-weakening glide of his fingers against the soaked panel of her panties. "And hot."

Sammi fumbled with his belt, needing his skin on hers. "These must go."

With a throaty laugh, Oliver pushed aside her hands and stripped off the rest of his clothes. She watched the process with avid delight as she backed toward the bed and settled onto the mattress. When he was naked, he stalked toward her. A primal pleasure lanced through her as he settled between her spread thighs, his heavy weight a warm blanket that made her tremble. He caught her wrists and held them above her head.

Sammi squirmed beneath him as his erection skimmed along her inner thigh. His mouth was back on her breast, his hand sliding over her soft stomach.

"Oliver."

She groaned as he dipped his fingers into the wet, swollen flesh that throbbed between her thighs. Crying out as he circled her clit before toying with her entrance, she thought she might do him harm if he didn't…

"Ah, yes."

They both gusted out a satisfied breath as he slid his finger into her.

"You are so sexy like this."

She was too far gone for his words to make her self-conscious. She closed her eyes and surrendered to the pleasure building beneath his masterful touch. Each glide and sweep brought her closer. She pushed against his hand, rocking to heighten the sensations. He planted a hot, openmouthed kiss on her lips, driving his tongue into her mouth as his fingers moved faster and harder.

Sammi's fingernails sank into his shoulder as she detonated against his hand. She bit down on his lip an instant before she came and then her mouth flew open as a cry broke from her throat, a harsh, ecstatic wrench of joy that made her laugh.

"Holy hell." Oliver kissed her softly, grinning with delight against her lips. "You are incredible."

"Tell me what you want to do next," she coaxed, smiling at him in bold satisfaction.

"I want to be inside you," he said. "To lose myself in your tight heat."

"I'm all yours."

With her body still shuddering with carnal aftershocks, Sammi lifted her hips and offered herself to him. His eyes softened and warmed as he acknowledged her invitation. She wanted him to understand how badly she needed him. That he was as important to her as the oxygen she breathed.

As he nipped and kissed his way along her neck, his hands gripped hers, their fingers meshing as he settled between her thighs. Captive beneath him, opened and waiting for his possession, Sammi knew no man suited her the way this one did.

"Your turn," she murmured.

"Oh, no," he responded. "This is our turn."

She smiled as he pressed into her, gliding through her slick arousal, stretching and filling her. This made sense. They made sense. In this moment. In this way. They belonged together. She threw back her head and took all of him in, shocked by an intense sense of belonging.

"Oliver—" Her voice broke on his name, overwhelmed by bliss as he filled her, slowly at first, taking his time, letting her adapt to his length. "Oh…"

He thrust into her deep and slow, the delirious, steady rhythm ripping a series of impassioned moans from her chest. Lips parting, she snatched air into her lungs until his mouth covered hers. Their tongues tangled as their bodies danced. He freed her hands and cupped her butt in his palms, shifting the angle of her hips so she could take him deeper still. Just when she thought it was impossible for the sensations to sharpen, he slipped his hand between them and touched her clit.

With a breathless cry she drove her nails into his shoulders, arched her back, and let him have all of her. Pleasure built, so acute it brought tears to her eyes. She was so close to letting go, so close to flying.

"I need to see you come," he gasped, body quaking as he kept his strokes even and let her orgasm build. "To watch you let go."

She opened her eyes, and there was no hiding from Oliver's hot blue gaze as her climax caught her up in a frenzy of pleasure. Lust and love collided in an incandescent explosion as Oliver and his hunger propelled her hard and fast into delirious ecstasy that tore the roof off her world and shot her straight to the stars.

In the aftermath, Sammi lay on her back, arms splayed, eyes on the ceiling as she sifted through her emotions. To her surprise she was steadier than she'd expected.

"Well, that went okay," she said, retreating into a place of reflection.

With her pregnancy giving their connection a level of permanence she hadn't planned for, she worried that the earth-shattering sex she was having with Oliver would leave her physically satisfied but emotionally hollow. She wasn't sure she could embrace desire without getting caught up in the intense emotion that accompanied the pleasure.

"I think it was better than okay," he pointed out, eyeing her. "In fact, I thought it was pretty freaking awesome."

"Definitely okay."

He rolled onto his side and propped his head on his hand, surveying her features without rancor. Hooking his fingers over her hip, he turned her to face him. "Is there something I missed?" A cocky grin tugged at the corners of his lips. "I know a lot of guys who are clueless when a woman is faking, but I think what you had was what's known as a screaming—"

She pressed her fingers against his lips to stop his words. "I know what I had."

"Then why aren't you happy?"

"Who says I'm not?" In fact, she was too overwhelmed to let it all out.

"You aren't giving me a satisfied-woman vibe right about now."

She didn't like the idea that he knew what that sort of vibe looked like. But he was wrong about her. She was satisfied. Just not comfortable enough to show him how much.

"I am satisfied." Very satisfied. In fact, she wanted to start all over again with the kissing and sex talk. And ride his big beautiful body into the wee hours.

"But…" he prompted, amusement threading his voice.

"But there's something else going on." She paused. "I'm not sure you'll be happy if I voice it."

"Let me start," he offered. "We're attracted to each other."

"And we're having a baby, so that's complicated."

"I don't know what happens next," Oliver admitted, "but I'd like to keep doing more of this while we figure it out."

But for how long?

She smiled. "I'd like that too."

"So, move in with me."

As tempting as it was to believe that this was a fairy tale come true, Sammi's instincts warned her that it was all happening too fast and for the wrong reasons. She'd promised herself that for her baby she'd make the right choices. No matter how hard those decisions were, unless she embraced her needs and stuck to her values, she'd continue to drift through life instead of being in charge.

"It's a big step," she murmured. And one fraught with all sorts of pitfalls. "I need a little time to think about it."

"Okay, I get it."

And that was that. After a casual peck on her cheek, Oliver gathered her body against his. He nuzzled his face into her neck, and before long, his breathing deepened into sleep. Snuggled against his solid frame, Sammi stared at the ceiling and, for this moment only, let herself believe this was exactly where she needed to be.

Eight

Oliver headed across the river and entered New Jersey on his way to lunch with his brother Joshua. He had a lot on his mind. Foremost was the situation with Sammi and his impending fatherhood. Parenting was a lifelong commitment of the sort he'd never contemplated making. Oliver had no illusions about himself or his character. He was a selfish bastard, far more likely to take than to give and no one's idea of a role model.

And as if all that wouldn't work against him, his childhood lacked the sort of touching family moments for him to draw on for inspiration. Yet he'd decided to reach out to Josh. To share his news, hoping the soul-searching that Joshua had gone through with his own paternity claim might help Oliver put his fears into perspective.

Until recently the gossipmongers had assumed Josh was the father of a four-year-old girl. DNA results and an anonymous source had pointed the finger straight at Joshua. After an extensive search for the mother and child among his former lovers, Josh denied being the child's father, a claim that Oliver took at face value. After all, Josh had been the one who'd taken on the role of hero by stepping up and pulling the family back from the brink of ruin.

Oliver was hoping that even though Josh hadn't turned out to be the father, he could sympathize with the emotional roller coaster that Oliver was on right now. Or maybe Josh would call him out as a self-involved asshole, unfit to be a parent. And maybe that's what Oliver was hoping to hear. Wouldn't his brother's criticism give him the perfect out? A sensible explanation for why he'd never push for partial custody. Sammi and the baby would be better off without him, right? She had enough drama in her life where her mother was concerned and didn't need the added trouble of Oliver and the chaos currently barging into his world. Surely everyone would be better off if he offered only financial support.

Driving into the town of Falling Brook, Oliver was struck by a mixed bag of emotions. How many of these stately homes with their manicured lawns and luxury cars parked in their driveways concealed dysfunctional families? That everything appeared perfect didn't mean it was. Look at all that went down with his family. From the outside looking in, no doubt everybody believed the Lowells had perfect lives. All the money they could ever spend. Attractive. Intelligent. Talented. Whatever any of them touched turned to gold. Fool's gold, maybe. Because the entire family had been made a fool of by Vernon Lowell.

Oliver passed the local prep school, recalling the trouble he'd gotten into there and the teachers that had encouraged him. Shaped by both good and bad experiences, he'd been completely unprepared for the challenges he would face when he left.

Parking his car beside the restaurant where he'd agreed

to meet Joshua, with a sick feeling in his gut that diminished his appetite, Oliver entered the building. He'd arrived before Joshua and slid into a seat near the back. A smiling waiter approached, and Oliver ordered a club soda with lime. Five minutes later, his brother wove through the restaurant, his tall, muscular frame encased in a well-tailored navy suit. Where Oliver's appearance was rough around the edges, Joshua was impeccably groomed and elegantly stylish.

With an amiable-enough greeting, Joshua slid into a chair opposite Oliver, his hazel-green gaze fixing on the crystal tumbler the waiter had just set before his brother. Out of habit, Oliver tensed. The need to defend himself jumped to the forefront, but he remained silent even as irritation rolled through him.

Joshua was so intent on the drink that he failed to note his brother's scowl. "I'll have what he's having," he said, indicating Oliver's choice.

When the waiter delivered the asked-for "cocktail," Oliver leaned back and waited for his brother to take his first sip. The resentment burning in his chest turned to harsh satisfaction as Joshua registered surprise when he tasted no alcohol.

"Club soda with a twist of lime," Oliver pointed out, choosing to feed his anger rather than set it aside. "My drink of choice."

That his brother thought the worst of him convinced Oliver to wait before discussing Sammi and the baby. If Joshua assumed he was incapable of maintaining his sobriety, then why would he believe that Oliver was qualified to be a good father?

"I thought maybe you'd…" Josh looked abashed.

"Fallen off the wagon?" Oliver quizzed, his lips twisting into a sardonic smile. "With everything that's going on,

my sobriety has been sorely tested, but I'm doing okay."
More than okay with Sammi in his life. Despite the looming chaos of his father's trial, Oliver was looking forward
to what his future held.

"Has Dad's attorney reached out to you?"

Oliver nodded. "Yes."

The attorney had left several messages about Vernon's
eagerness to have his sons visit the prison where he was
awaiting trial. That his father arrogantly assumed he could
summon them after fifteen years of silence made Oliver's
blood boil.

"Are you going to see him?"

"No." He studied his brother, remembering Vernon's
pride in his eldest son. To his surprise, there was no sign
of the envy that usually afflicted Oliver when he recalled
those days. "How about you?"

"I haven't decided." Josh looked grim. "There are days
I wish he'd—" Oliver's brother broke off and swallowed
hard "—never been found."

"How are things going with Black Crescent now that
Vernon has reappeared?"

"I'm worried his trial is going to mess up all the good
work we've managed to do in the company's name." With
Josh at the helm, Black Crescent had repaired its tarnished
image through community outreach, donations made to
various nonprofits and reparations made or attempted toward affected families. "And the media circus surrounding
his capture and trial is making my search for Black Crescent's next CEO impossible."

"So it's not going well?"

Josh shook his head. "My top picks have turned us down.
At this point I'm unsure if we'll ever find a suitable replace-
ment." Oliver's brother looked like a man who was staring
at a bleak future. He cradled his drink between his palms

and glared at the contents as if wishing it were something stronger than bubbly water. "Even though you told me you don't have the best track record, I don't suppose you'd be interested in the job?"

Oliver laughed. "Oh, hell no. When I said that, it was my way of politely declining. I love my job, and I'm good at it."

His brother's emphatic response made Josh smirk. Almost immediately, however, his amusement faded back to melancholy. "You know I really envy what you've done with your life."

Given that Josh had assumed his brother's drink had contained alcohol, Oliver snorted. "You don't say."

"You followed your passion. Your photography is amazing. And you get to do what you love." Joshua had given up his art so he could be the man of the family.

"Did you forget the part where I was kicked out of Harvard, and then spent the next five years drunk and high until I was nearly beaten to death when I was trying to score?" Because Oliver was pretty sure Josh hadn't.

"No." Joshua's expression soured. "You were a screwup back then, but you've changed. In fact, you might be the most successful of us all."

Oliver stared at his brother in open astonishment. Would Josh still believe that once he learned that Oliver was going to be a father?

"After Dad disappeared," Oliver began, "why didn't you just turn your back on the company and keep going with your art?"

He'd always perceived Joshua as the brother who was the most together. He had done the right thing while Jake ran away and Oliver descended into addiction.

"Believe me, I wanted to be selfish, but someone had to look after Mom and the company."

Oliver knew Josh's disdainful tone was directed at his

absent twin, who'd refused to change his plans to backpack through Europe after their father disappeared with the millions he'd stolen from Black Crescent. Even if he'd had an aptitude for business, Oliver had been far too young running a multimillion-dollar hedge fund.

"Did you resent having to step up while the rest of us got to do what we wanted?"

"You mean did it bother me that both you and Jake scoffed at me for following in dear old Dad's footsteps and didn't appreciate that I gave up my dream for a life I never wanted in order to take care of Mom?"

"Yeah," Oliver murmured. "That."

Joshua's lips twisted into a sardonic smile. "Not at first. In the beginning I was able to point to all of you and revel in how I was doing the right thing. I viewed the sacrifices I made as my success and your failure." Josh shook his head. "But what did I get for my pride? I was miserable and alone. It kept me from reaching out to you, to Jake. I put up walls and was surprised when no one wanted to climb over them."

To think that Josh, always known as the "good" twin, had suffered because of the choices he'd made was something Oliver would spend time wrapping his head around. It had never occurred to him that his brother might have regrets.

"So what are your plans after you step down as CEO?" Oliver asked, turning their conversation from the miserable past to a brighter future.

"I'm going to focus on things that make me happy."

"It seems like you already have that covered with Sophie."

Sophie Armstrong had burst into Joshua's life while writing an anniversary piece on the "Black Crescent Fiasco." The article turned out to be filled with wild theories and blatant inaccuracies about the Lowell family, especially Joshua. In the process of digging for background information, Sophie learned about Joshua's supposed illegitimate child, but she never published the information. Instead she told Joshua what she'd discovered. Confronted with a DNA report, Joshua had contacted every woman from his past and found none of them had a four-year-old girl they claimed was his. Despite keeping it out of the article, the rumor mill got a hold of it, and everyone in Falling Brook knew.

"She is the best thing that ever happened to me," Josh agreed. "When everyone else was convinced the DNA test was legitimate and that I was refusing to acknowledge that little girl as mine, Sophie believed me when I said I would never do that. And I wouldn't."

His brother's fervent declaration resonated with Oliver. "Have you figured out what's up with the DNA test?"

"I checked out the doctor who ran the test. Although he's pretty shady, turns out his results are accurate." Joshua paused for effect, and a smile ghosted across his lips. "Jake is the father."

"You're sure?

"As sure as an identical twin can be," Josh said. "And I wish I could say I'm surprised that Jake hasn't come forward to claim her."

"Have you heard from him?"

"Not a word."

Both men sat in silence for several minutes while Oliver processed what he'd learned. The waiter chose that moment to appear and take their order. After he left, Joshua settled his serious gaze on Oliver. "I'm sure you didn't invite me to lunch to chat with me about my love life or Black Crescent. Or even our dad. So, Ol, what's on your mind?"

"You know that conversation we had where we both agreed that we'd be disasters as dads?" Oliver paused and let a few of their choice remarks replay in his head. "And how I went on and on about how I never wanted the responsibility of fatherhood?"

He let his voice trail off and waited for his meaning to sink in. When Joshua's eyes narrowed, Oliver braced himself for his brother's censure.

"You're going to be a father?" Joshua asked, his tone neutral.

Oliver exhaled. "Yes."

"You look as if you expect me to scold you about it. Well, those days are over. You're a grown-ass man, and as such you need to take responsibility. But I think you already know that." Joshua's tone hit the perfect note, and Oliver smiled. "So what can I help you with?"

"I plan on taking responsibility for the child. To do anything else has never been an option. But I've been thinking a lot about what we talked about." Oliver braced himself and asked the question that had plagued him since learning Sammi was pregnant. "Did you mean it when you said you'd make a terrible father? Was that just blowing off steam because you knew the child wasn't yours?" Oliver could see from his brother's flat expression that he wasn't doing a good job communicating the angst that filled him. "When you say doing the right thing, are you talking about financial support or really stepping up and being a great dad?"

"I guess when I was in the thick of the situation and believing it was possible for me to be the child's father, I was so caught up in finding the mother and child that I didn't spend a lot of time thinking what would happen when I did."

With everything that Joshua had been through in the last few months, Oliver wasn't surprised that his brother would prioritize actual problems over abstract improbabilities.

"And now that you and Sophie are together, have you thought about having children?"

"To be honest, I know we will, but I haven't considered what sort of dad I'd be." Joshua wore a contemplative frown, as if Oliver's questions had opened Pandora's box. "I'm sorry if that doesn't help you."

"That's okay," Oliver said, hiding his disappointment. "This really is something I need to sort out for myself."

"Who's the woman?" Joshua asked. "Have you been seeing her for a while?"

"Samantha Guzman. Sammi. We only met recently—right after I received that fishing equipment—and I wasn't thinking clearly that night."

Joshua gave him an understanding nod. "Are you together?"

"It's complicated," Oliver admitted. "The thing is, I like her a lot. In fact, I asked her to move in with me. But I have no idea where things are going, and it's not as if I ever imagined going the whole traditional-relationship route with a commitment and possibly marriage."

"Neither did I, until Sophie came along."

"But it's different with me. I've never been the guy that other people could rely on. I'm not romantic, and most everyone who has dealt with me at one point or another thinks I'm a pain-in-the-ass jerk. And if all that isn't bad enough, then Vernon had to get himself spotted on that Caribbean island and extradited back here to face trial. Maybe if that hadn't happened, I could've eventually closed the door on my past. But now he's reappeared, and the amount of media this has stirred up is driving me crazy."

Oliver paused in his tirade and unclenched his fists. The rage that swept him every time he thought about how his father had been living it up in style all these years while they all suffered made him want to throw things. He took several deep breaths until he could continue on a calmer note.

"I don't want to drag Sammi or our baby into this mess. Part of me thinks she'd be better off without me. Both of them would be."

His chest seized at the thought of not seeing her every day. How could he survive not waking up with her in his arms, her beautiful brown eyes soft and warm as she watched him blink sleep away? He wanted to share the day's adventures over dinner and make love into the wee hours of the night. To be around for every stage of her pregnancy and experience every first their baby went through.

"Dad won't be front-page news forever," Josh said, his gaze thoughtful. "We'll all get through this. Even Mom is doing better than I thought she would be. I saw her this morning. I expected a repeat of the depression spiral from fifteen years ago. Instead she made me tea and told me we'd get through this too. She's come a long way. Ol, don't let Dad ruin another good thing in your life."

"But what if I'm the one who ruins it?" Oliver had resisted facing this anxiety for too long. "I fight my addiction every day. It's a battle I'll be in for the rest of my life. What if I slip up? When I get stressed, the struggle increases tenfold. Sammi deserves better than to get trapped into a relationship with someone she can't trust and can't count on."

"Do you really think she can't trust or count on you?" Joshua asked. "Or are you just using your addiction as an excuse to avoid trying your hardest?"

Was that what he was doing? The last eight years had been hard, but except for a couple of slipups early on, he'd maintained his sobriety. Nor had he used his addiction to avoid doing something challenging. Starting now seemed a failure in itself.

"Not to mention," Josh continued, "that you're ignoring all the good she could do for you. Of course, you'd have to let her help, and that's not exactly the easiest thing for us Lowell brothers to accept."

Sammi stood in her closet, sorting through her wardrobe and her feelings for Oliver in light of his invitation to move in. She'd asked for a few days to consider his offer and, thanks to a long list of pros and cons, continued to grapple with the decision. In the meantime, and without anyone's help, she'd located a temporary rental but hadn't yet committed to it. The studio apartment was in an area Oliver would find acceptable and the size of an average hotel room. Though it was smaller than anything she'd lived in since her modeling career had taken off, the low rent offered her the ability to save up for when the baby came. Accomplishing this on her own had given her a boost of confidence. And provided an option if she decided not to move in with Oliver.

Abruptly the playlist Sammi had been listening to ended, and she became aware of the silent apartment. Her mother had moved out, taking the tense atmosphere with her, but the resulting emptiness filled Sammi with sadness and regret. She'd been so resentful of Celeste for driving her modeling career that Sammi had lost touch with their bond as mother and daughter. She would love to talk to her mother about moving in with Oliver, but she knew Celeste's advice would be to get a big fat financial settlement from him, enough to set her and the baby up for life. Weeks earlier this might have irritated Sammi no end, but she was starting to understand her mother's paranoia about being poor.

Today's video shoot with Kimberly's fiancé had given her a much-needed reality check. The answer she'd received about the chances of making much income off this fledgling idea had dimmed her enthusiasm about the project, but she was determined to give it all she had. Who knew what opportunities might arise from it, and Sammi needed to be open to any that presented themselves.

Which brought her back to the idea of moving in with Oliver. The decision would've been easier if she hadn't slept with him again. Before that happened, she could've kept things strictly platonic, moved into his guest room, and pretended that she was immune to his sexy gorgeousness and the glimpses of sweetness that appeared like sunshine amid the dark clouds of his gruff exterior.

If she hadn't succumbed to temptation, she wouldn't be worried about what would happen when he tired of having her in his bed. Her thoughts turned to that twenty-three-dollar photo session that he still owed her. They never discussed it, and Sammi was starting to feel superstitious about what would happen if they followed through. When he'd initially offered the trade, she hadn't thought beyond sharing a few personal thoughts, after which she'd received a portrait that would reveal her nature.

These days, her mind linked the photo with the end of her connection to Oliver. A ridiculous notion, since she was pregnant with his child. Sammi traced her fingers over her still-flat belly. She wasn't a temporary fixture in his life. But on days when pregnancy hormones twisted up her emotions, Sammi wondered if she would continue to interest Oliver once he knew everything there was about her.

As if he sensed she was thinking about him, her phone buzzed with a text.

Want to have dinner?

Joy blazed through her, leaving giddiness in its wake. Since he'd gone to see his brother, she hadn't expected he'd be in the mood for company afterward. From what he'd shared with her about growing up with twin older brothers and how all three siblings had been estranged since the scandal surrounding their father's hedge fund, she'd imagined that he wouldn't be in any mood for company.

Sammi engaged the reply box and began to type.

I'd love to.

Before she sent that message, she considered what she'd typed. Although *love* was the right word, it came off as too strong and too eager. She tried again.

What time are you thinking?

How about now? There's a car waiting downstairs. I have a surprise for you.

Sammi rolled her eyes. While Oliver's impulsiveness often thrilled her, sometimes she wished he didn't assume she would drop whatever she was doing to be with him. This led her to ponder their different parenting styles. No doubt he would be a fun one, the dad who tickled and played right before nap time, leaving her to be the serious parent left to calm their child for sleep.

As this scenario played out in her mind, Sammi noted that in her mind they were co-parenting while living together. This made her sigh in mingled wistfulness and vexation. She had to stop imagining herself deeply entrenched in his life.

Their cohabitation could evolve into almost anything. Yet so far she'd resisted the temptation to ask him to define what was happening. Did he view her as someone he wanted to spend his life with? Was he content to drift along for years with no spoken commitment binding them together?

And what was she after? Oliver's inner landscape was a lot more complicated than she'd ever imagined. He avoided discussing his relationship with his family, leaving her to wonder if it was terrible or nonexistent. Rage filled him anytime his father's name was mentioned. And as if the anger wasn't unsettling enough, it was often followed by lengthy brooding silences that left her feeling lost and on the outside looking in. As much as she wanted more than anything to help him cope with all the bad feelings, her response to being shut out was to withdraw in kind.

How could two such damaged people ever be in a healthy relationship? As much as she wanted to reach through the darkness and connect with Oliver, she didn't know if she was strong enough to weather his emotional storms. Realizing he was waiting for her to answer, Sammi answered the irresistible call of her heart and typed a reply.

Give me 10 minutes.

She quickly changed into something more flattering than worn leggings and the T-shirt emblazoned with *GRL PWR* that she'd donned to tackle her closet. Clad in skinny jeans and an oversize black sweater, hair swept into a messy top-knot, she headed downstairs.

When the elevator doors opened on the lobby, the first thing that greeted her was an enormous stuffed giraffe and, beside the long neck, Oliver's handsome face, wearing the most charming smile she'd seen to date. At the sight her pulse skipped a beat.

"What's this?" she asked, warning herself to rein it back.

It wasn't his fault that she found him irresistible. Well, that wasn't quite true. If he would just stop being so damned charismatic, maybe she could gather the strength to resist him. Why could the man always get under her skin?

"It's the first decoration for our baby's nursery. I thought we could go pick out some furniture."

"It's really cute, but I'm not even two months along." To her dismay, tears sprang to her eyes. Damn her pregnancy hormones and the way her hopes skyrocketed at the picture of enthusiastic fatherhood that he presented. "Don't you think it's too early?"

His eager smile faded. "I thought you'd be excited to start decorating the nursery."

The speed at which Oliver was moving into her life left her no room to reason or plan. She hadn't yet decided to move in with him, and the pressure to make him happy by agreeing made her chest tighten.

"I am."

"But?" He'd obviously heard her reluctance.

All her life Sammi had acted in a practical manner, working to support her and her mother when she'd probably rather have played with friends and worried about her grades and what boys liked her. Was it so unreasonable that she'd refuse to accept less than exactly what she longed for?

"I'm absolutely starving." She wrapped her arm around his and turned him toward the front entrance. "Didn't you say something about dinner?"

Nine

Although Oliver was disappointed that Sammi hadn't enthusiastically embraced his plans for creating a nursery in his guest bedroom, he realized that he shouldn't be surprised, given that she'd shown more concern than delight about his proposal that they cohabitate.

Oliver took her to a tiny, dimly lit restaurant that featured Basque-inspired French and Spanish dishes, where Sammi demonstrated that she was as hungry as she claimed. As an array of small plates arrived at their table, she pounced upon the *boquerones* on toast and cremini mushrooms with chorizo and garlic cream, attacking the food with gusto, licking her lips and groaning in a way that made Oliver's jeans grow overly snug. Despite the discomfort, he savored every second of the meal.

The peaceful evening continued until they returned to his apartment, carrying the large giraffe with them. When they stepped into the foyer, the stuffed toy became the elephant in the room as it raised the specter of their disagreement over starting to design the nursery. Since sex was an excellent diversion, he deposited the plush animal on a barstool before sweeping Sammi off her feet and carrying her to the bedroom.

They made love with energetic abandon, their bodies communicating without doubt or hesitation. Oliver wished everything was as easy with Sammi, but they were a pair of islands, accustomed to solitude, finding it easier to hide from the world's harshness than open up and invite rejection. In his case, he'd avoided his family and the place where he'd grown up yet had never truly fit in. Hating the isolation, he'd numbed his pain first with drugs and then with work, leaving no room for relationships that might end badly. He used physical distance and sardonic disdain to keep others at bay while she kept her emotions hidden behind a passive exterior.

Yet they'd gravitated toward each other.

With aftershocks reverberating through him, Oliver murmured in gratitude that fate had brought this woman into his life. She lay draped across his chest, a sated, boneless weight that made him smile. He swept his fingertips along her spine as their bodies cooled. Not until goose bumps broke out on her skin and she shivered did he move to pull the comforter over them.

"How did your visit go with your brother?" she asked, her cheek on his shoulder, one slim thigh thrown over his. "What is Falling Brook like?"

Oliver felt her curiosity as well as her concern. He'd confessed his reservations about the town where he'd faced so many disappointments.

"Every time I go there, I can't stop feeling hostile. There's too many bad memories." Even though he'd left Falling Brook feeling optimistic about the future, he couldn't stop himself from brooding about what had happened in the past. Maybe that's why as soon as he got his first big paycheck he bought a house in Falling Brook, to show everyone he wasn't a failure. No one questioned why he was never there. "Josh can't let go of his opinion of me as the messed-up kid brother who got hooked on drugs and made everybody's life miserable."

"Did he say that?"

"No." But Oliver recalled how Josh had questioned his sobriety by ordering the same drink. "But Josh made it pretty clear that he doesn't trust me not to fall into old habits."

"Oh."

A quick glance at her expression told him he'd given her something to worry about. He gave himself a mental kick. Stress wasn't good for her or the baby. She had enough on her plate without him dumping his problems on her.

"I'm sorry." Seeing how his outburst had affected her, he tamped down his impatience. To win her trust he needed her to believe he was okay. "I didn't mean to upset you."

Through their connection, he felt her muscles twitch and heard her deep exhalation. As she relaxed, Oliver's last bit of irritation bled away.

"You didn't."

"I'm in full control of my addiction." But these were stressful times, and he hadn't been perfect these last eight years. "I won't mess up. I swear."

Her soft smile lit up his world. "I'm not worried."

The burning glow that filled his chest at her transparent faith filled him with tranquility and optimism. Feeling the connection with her deepen, he brushed his lips over hers.

"I always feel so much better when I'm around you."

She regarded him through her lashes. "I'm glad."

Although Oliver recognized that she hadn't echoed his

sentiment, he knew he couldn't blame her. In this way he was very much like his father, selfish and prone to doing as he pleased and to hell with how it affected everyone around him.

They lapsed into an easy silence, and Oliver didn't realize he'd dozed off until he awoke to find his bed empty. Panic brought him to full wakefulness. He sat up, but as soon as he noticed that their clothes were neatly piled on a nearby chair, he slid out of bed and went in search of her. She hadn't gone far, merely next door to his guest room.

Standing in the open doorway, wearing his T-shirt and nothing else, she was studying the room before her. He slowly approached, lingering to admire her long legs and imagining his hands riding the lean muscles of her thighs to the hot, wet space between. No doubt his harsh breathing announced his arrival, because she glanced over her shoulder in his direction.

"It's empty," she remarked as he slid his arms around her waist from behind. Sighing, she relaxed against his chest and drew absent circles on his forearms.

"Think of it as a blank slate," he countered, inhaling the scent of sex and sweat that mingled with lavender on her skin.

"This is happening so fast."

Fingertips skimming her nape, he brushed her hair aside and set his lips on her shoulder. She gasped and trembled.

"When there's something I want, I go after it."

He coasted his hands along her curves, letting her warmth seep into him. She was everything to him. The more time he spent with her, the more he craved her company. Holding her hand calmed his spirit. Making her come filled his world with joy.

"I know it's early," she began, her voice husky and low as his lips drifted over her skin, "but I think we should talk about what happens after the baby's born. Specifically, how do you see this co-parenting thing working for us?"

While he knew she was being sensible, her question made tension twist in his gut. "You know how I feel. I think we should live together so our child will have both parents around all the time."

He played his fingertips beneath the T-shirt and skimmed over her belly, making the muscles dance in response. Need spread heat beneath his skin even as she caught his hand and stilled it.

"While that sounds ideal," she responded, her voice breathless and raw as he tugged the T-shirt off, "I'm not convinced that we shouldn't consider alternatives."

"Wouldn't it be better to focus on what's best for our child?" His heart beat in erratic time, matching the unruly shudders that racked her as he found her breast and lightly pinched the nipple.

"We need an arrangement that works for all of us." Her words picked up speed as if she wanted to get everything out before he could distract her past the point of thought.

He was already close. Cupping his hand over her mound, he pressed her back into him. With her gorgeous butt trapping his hard length between them, he was nearly mindless with lust. Her fingernail bit into his thigh as he slid the head of his erection against her backside, thrusting against her, letting the friction drive his desire higher. A shock wave trembled through her as he eased his fingers between her thighs and teased her the way she liked with a combination of gentle caresses and deeper strokes.

"One week on, one week off," she panted, her voice a near whimper as she rocked against his hand. "Or alternating nights during the week. You have a busy travel schedule, so I imagine that we would have to work around that."

None of this sounded appealing in the least. He didn't

want their child shuffled from apartment to apartment. Determined to put an end to the conversation, Oliver spun her around and pinned her hands over her head.

"Let's talk about this later," he said, calming his voice even as his emotions raged. Fighting with her would only create the sort of distance between them that would grow over time. He stared into her passion-heavy gaze. "Right now all I want to think about is us."

Hearing the impassioned groan that wrenched from her lips as he lifted her off her feet, he captured her mouth in a hard, demanding kiss. A heartbeat later, she wrapped her legs around his thighs and they melded in a rhapsody of aching pleasure and blissful sighs.

Although Sammi had several gowns that might have suited, since she was going as Oliver's date, the dress she selected had to make the perfect statement. With all the attention he was receiving from the media since his father had been apprehended and thrown in prison, she wanted to be memorable, but not flashy. Yet while making fashion decisions was in her comfort zone, tonight she was bound to be asked about their relationship, and Sammi remained unsure if she was ready to claim that they were a couple.

At least she was confident in her choice of a black cocktail dress of organza with an overlay of black lace-edged tulle for the party. The strapless design and full skirt were a glamorous fifties-inspired retro look that Sammi heightened by styling her hair in a smooth chignon with soft tendrils framing her face. Simple crystal drop earrings completed the look.

When she opened the door and saw Oliver standing outside her apartment, she tried not to gawk at the way his formal wear enhanced his broad shoulders and turned him into an elegant stranger.

She'd never even seen him in a suit and had no idea he owned a tuxedo. His usual attire of jeans, shirts and leather jackets gave his blond all-American good looks an edgy quality that suited his big-city bad-boy image. His rough edges let everyone forget that he'd grown up in the exclusive bedroom community of Falling Brook, New Jersey, with a mansion filled with staff to tend to his every need. Utterly comfortable in perfectly tailored Tom Ford, Oliver looked every inch a man of wealth beyond anything she could wrap her head around and highlighted the differences in their upbringing.

He must've picked up on her sudden uneasiness. "What's wrong?"

"Nothing." Sammi took his arm and tried to escort him toward the door, but he planted his feet and refused to move. Finally, she gave up with a sigh. "I'm just a little bit nervous about tonight."

Initially thrilled that he'd invited her to the party, as she selected the perfect dress, she'd started wondering what to say when people asked about their relationship. They spent so much time alone that she hadn't given much thought to labeling what was progressing between them. Tonight's event was different. Before this, Oliver had maintained a low profile where his dating life was concerned, and Sammi wasn't sure what her role was supposed to be. Did he want to admit they were dating? Living together? Future parents? Friends only?

"You have nothing to worry about," Oliver said, his deep voice reverberating through her.

"This is the first time we've attended a party together."

He tensed. "Are you worried about being the focus of bad publicity from being seen with me?"

"Hardly." She tightened her grip, fierce in her defense

of him, and wished she could voice what was really on her mind. "Are you sure I look okay?"

"You look gorgeous," he intoned, his deep voice sending pleasure rippling through her.

"Good," she murmured. "Because people are going to notice me on your arm."

To her shock, Oliver took her by the shoulders and stared down at her. "I hope you realize that no matter how you look, I will always be proud of you."

His utter seriousness curled her toes. She cupped his cheek, flushed with wonder. She loved that Oliver always treated her as someone he admired and cherished. The men she dated before him had all wanted her because of her beauty and didn't give a damn about her thoughts or feelings. They liked how she looked, not who she was. And while she recognized that Oliver was attracted to her beauty, what lurked below her surface appealed to him just as much.

"Even when I'm as big as a house and unable to see my feet?" she teased, her pulse racing as he skimmed his palms down her arms and took her hands in his.

"Especially then." He lifted first one palm and then the other and grazed kisses over her skin. "You're important to me."

Breathless with delight, she practically floated down the hall to the elevator and then across the lobby to where a town car awaited them. When Oliver slid in beside her, Sammi snuggled against his side, absorbing his heat and breathing in his spicy masculine aftershave.

"You smell good," she sighed on a soft purr.

"Keep that up and I'll be tempted to skip the party and take you back home."

Sammi delighted in his threat, regretting that she let her nerves get the better of her earlier. Why couldn't she just enjoy how well they were getting along and not expect anything more? Of course, thanks to her pregnancy, she couldn't pretend that their connection was complication-free. Where most couples had months or years to decide about the future with a baby coming, Sammi needed to figure out where she and Oliver stood sooner rather than later.

They spoke little during the drive from her Midtown apartment to the Upper East Side penthouse where the party was taking place. Sammi's excitement about the evening ahead was only matched by her nervousness. She'd attended several after-parties during New York fashion weeks, but never on the arm of someone as well-known as Oliver Lowell.

His large hand warmed the small of her back as he guided her through the foyer and into the large formal living room. With Oliver beside her, she was less daunted by the sea of unfamiliar faces than she'd imagined. And except for some bland pleasantries, she didn't have to offer much in the way of conversation.

Everyone they met had only one thing they wanted to talk about: how Oliver was handling the shocking reappearance of his father after an absence of fifteen years. Sammi was impressed how smoothly Oliver handled the inquiries without giving away his true feelings. If she hadn't seen firsthand how much the situation upset him, she might have believed that he was as nonchalant as he appeared.

After they'd been circulating for over an hour, Sammi slipped away for a much-needed restroom break, and when she returned to look for Oliver, she found him deep in discussion with a group of men. Deciding not to interrupt, Sammi headed out the French doors for a breath of air and crossed the small terrace to the iron railing. The view of New York City at night was spectacular from the eighteenth floor. She shivered in the late October chill but refused to go back inside until she'd drunk her fill of the myriad of lights.

"Hello." A slender blonde in a hot-pink Valentino gown sidled up to Sammi. She affected the languid expression of a socialite who'd attended far too many of these sorts of functions and found them utterly tedious. "I noticed you're with Oliver. Did he bring you to this event?"

"Yes."

"You look familiar." The blonde puckered her pink lips as her expression grew thoughtful. "But I know all of Oliver's friends, and I'm sure we've never met."

Sammi scrutinized the attractive blonde and wondered if this was one of Oliver's former lovers or someone he'd photographed. Maybe both?

"That's probably because we've only known each other a few weeks," Sammi said.

"Are you two dating?" The woman had been sizing up Sammi in turn, evaluating her fashion choice through narrowed green eyes.

Unsure how to answer, Sammi sent her gaze darting toward the French doors in the hope that Oliver might come looking for her and broadcasted a silent plea for rescue.

"We're friends," she explained, hoping the careful answer would satisfy the woman's curiosity.

"Of course. Oliver doesn't date." The blonde went on as if Sammi hadn't spoken. "Lots of women have tried and failed to hold his interest. Once he gets you all figured out, he tends to move on."

Sammi thought about that photograph that he'd never taken of her and her belief that her appeal would be diminished once his curiosity was satisfied. When he'd invited her to move in, he gave her clear reasons why this would benefit them both. But that was before they'd rekindled their physical relationship. Was she a fool to think that sex would add dimension to his purpose for keeping her around? Could he develop feelings for her that had nothing to do with the fact that she was expecting his child?

The familiar scent of Oliver's cologne brushed her senses as a tuxedo jacket settled over her bare shoulders. She gathered the lapels together, her skin tingling as Oliver's muscular frame became a solid presence at her side. The blonde's eyes went wide as his strong arm enfolded Sammi in a warm embrace.

"Hello, Bianca," he said. "I see you and Sammi have met."

"Sammi?" the blonde echoed, arching one eyebrow.

"Samantha Guzman," Sammi said, supplying her full name.

"I was just asking her if you two are dating," Bianca said, sending a crafty smile Oliver's way.

"And what did she say?" Oliver's fingers tightened in warning as Sammi drew in a sharp breath.

Bianca focused all her energy on Oliver, acting as if Sammi had ceased to exist. "I'm more interested in what you'd say."

While he appeared unimpressed by the blonde's games, Sammi was vibrating with dismay. She and Oliver should've coordinated their answers to the tricky questions that were sure to come their way. Still, she caught herself holding her breath in anticipation of what Oliver's answer might reveal.

"You know I don't talk about my personal business," Oliver said, neatly dodging the question. "But if you're wondering whether I'm off the market, then the answer is yes."

A mild earthquake rocked Sammi's equilibrium at Oliver's claim, leaving her a little dizzy. But then she noticed Bianca's scowl and understood that he'd intended to discourage the beautiful socialite.

"Have you ever been on the market?" Sammi murmured,

filling her tone with ironic humor as Bianca left them alone on the terrace.

His offhanded shrug admitted nothing. "What did you tell her about our relationship?"

"That we're friends." When he stiffened, nerves fluttered in her stomach. She tugged on his sleeve. "We are friends, right?"

"Is that all we are?"

Sammi quaked as his irritation flared. Wasn't "friends" a safe answer? They hadn't defined their relationship. What had he expected her to tell the curious woman with the sly green eyes?

"I don't know if that's all we are," Sammi said, her emotions churning. "We haven't talked about anything having to do with us."

"I asked you to move in. Isn't that proof that I want you in my life?"

Sammi was painfully aware that even though they were sleeping together, they were a couple by circumstance rather than choice.

"Yes, but because of the baby." She recalled what Bianca had said about his short attention span where women were concerned. "And you asked before we slept together again. I can't help but feel like we're rushing into something neither one of us is ready for."

"Is that really how you feel? Like you're not ready for what's happening between us?"

What was happening between them? They were fantastic in bed, but there was an indefinable something they were not willing to share with each other. They were letting sex be a substitute for intimacy.

"I think we both hold back."

"Maybe we should talk more about this." He glanced around. "But not here. Let's go."

Ten

Sammi's words preoccupied Oliver as they said goodbye to their host and left the party. He directed their driver to take them back to his loft. Although she hadn't officially agreed to move in, Sammi spent most nights with him. But when they reached his apartment, neither one of them was eager to talk. Instead, they ended up in his bedroom, communicating with lips and fingers as their bodies merged on his cool sheets in a rush of hungry desperation.

"That was amazing," she groaned beneath him, her chest heaving in unruly gasps.

Oliver braced himself on his elbows and slid the tips of his fingers through the sheen of perspiration dampening her soft cheek. Nothing moved him quite as deeply as witnessing Sammi giving herself over to a powerful orgasm. They might struggle to open up to each other outside the bedroom, but the same couldn't be said for their level of frankness while wrapped in each other's arms. He knew exactly what she liked, what drove her wild, and she trusted him to touch her in ways no other man had.

As he rolled onto his side and shifted her so they were both lying face-to-face, he noticed that her gaze eluded his. With passion melting away, their earlier conversation came back to haunt him. That she continued to doubt their relationship made something shift in his chest. He settled his hands beneath his head and stared at her beautiful face. Less than a foot separated them, but she seemed farther away than ever. Since asking her to move in, it was as if she'd been in a full-out retreat.

Couldn't she see that this was a huge step for him? He never imagined himself living with anyone, much less committing to being a father and immersing himself in the role. What more did she want?

He'd been counting on his offer to live with him being good enough to draw her in. Despite how brief their time together had been thus far, she was already an important fixture in his world. He thought about her all day long, missed her in the quiet moments. Most evenings he wooed her with delicious dinners or fun outings. Most nights they returned to his loft, ravenous for each other, and spent their time together lost in each other's arms.

She had clothes in his closet and her own space in his bathroom. His refrigerator was stocked with her favorite foods, and she had a key. It was like living together, except she hadn't changed her address or given up her apartment, even though her mother had moved out a week ago. Why was she resisting taking that next step? She used excuses like it was too fast or she didn't want to be a bother, but when he read between the lines, she was afraid he would lose interest in her as his lover and relegate her to the role of baby mama.

Well, he'd been giving that a lot of thought and had a

way to combine both roles in a way that would give her the stability she craved.

Oliver cupped her cheek in his palm and drew his thumb over her passion-bruised lips. "I think we should get married."

Sammi's eyes widened. "What? Why would you suggest something like that?"

Because if she was looking to slap a label on their relationship, husband and wife was the obvious choice. "It makes perfect sense."

"Sense?" she echoed, frowning. "How so?"

"We both get something that's important to us."

"I know what I want from a marriage. What is it you are looking for?"

"I think both of us can agree that we don't want our child to lack for anything."

"Of course, but we don't need to get married for that to happen."

"But I want us to be a family, and you're resisting moving in here." Although he'd never imagined himself tied down with anyone, he could see no better reason to get married than this. "It occurs to me that you need a commitment from me. So let's get married."

"Let me get this straight. You're only marrying me because I'm pregnant." From her quarrelsome tone, it seemed his justification had annoyed her.

"Is it wrong for me to want our child to have a sense of belonging that I never did?"

An almost imperceptible twitch of her eyebrow was Sammi's only response. In fact, she was so still that he swore she'd stopped breathing.

"What do you say?" he prompted, his voice tinged with exasperation as he realized she wasn't going to answer without prompting.

"What do you expect me to say?"

"Yes." He punctuated the word with an impatient gesture, unable to understand why she wasn't overjoyed at his proposal. Didn't she understand what he was offering? He wanted to marry her. Where was the enthusiastic hug and the impassioned kiss? Why wasn't she delighted?

What he got instead was a subdued tone and polite words. "I'm very happy that you want to be involved in our child's life." Her nostrils flared as she sucked in a deep breath. "But I don't want to marry you."

"Give me one reason why not."

"I barely know you." She pressed her lips together, and he wondered what else was on her mind.

"That's not true," he countered, thinking about everything he'd shared with her. "You know more about me than anyone."

Her lashes flickered as she considered his words. "I've been in committed relationships before, but this is the first time I actually want to be in one." When she spoke next, her voice was so low he could barely hear her. "But I've always imagined when I got married that it would be because we were in love."

She used the term "we" and he knew exactly what that meant.

"Are you asking me if I love you?" Oliver's annoyance flared as the muscles in his throat constricted. He wanted nothing to do with love. It caused nothing but pain.

"Of course not," Sammi said, seeming determined to thrust one obstacle after another between them. "How could you? As I said earlier, we barely know each other."

"But you won't get married without it." And Oliver wasn't a man who made promises he couldn't fulfill. "I can promise our child will be adored and supported by me."

Why couldn't she just be happy to be the woman he

wanted to spend the rest of his life with? Couples fell in love and got married all the time. That didn't mean they were going to make it. Wasn't it better if they were friends who respected and lusted after each other? That the only expectations between them were honesty and fidelity? His mother loved his father and he'd betrayed and abandoned her. How was that better than what Oliver was promising Sammi?

"I just don't get what's the big deal," Oliver said. "I'm willing to commit everything to you and our baby."

"Not everything," she argued. "Not what's important."

"What could possibly be more important than our child growing up having something I lacked?" He needed to make it clear that he'd never be satisfied as a part-time parent. "Something that neither one of us had. The love and support of two parents."

Her manner grew fierce as she insisted, "We'll give that to our child."

"I know we will, but wouldn't it be better if we didn't have two households?" he asked, backtracking when he realized he was letting his frustration get in the way of convincing her to marry him. "You said I'm not committed to what's important. What do you mean by that?"

They stared at each other in silence, the energy between them a clash of inflexible wills. Oliver's breath roughened as he fought down panic. In her eyes he saw the sort of determination that ran marathons, won gold medals and drove every underdog ever to get back to their feet after being knocked down.

"I'm falling in love with you." She spoke the words like a prayer. "And I can't imagine a future without you in it, but I can't marry you unless you're doing it for the right reasons. I need you to love me back. It's that simple."

She'd made her decision and showed no sign of relenting or retreat. Anger and despair clashed inside him as he realized it was up to him to decide how to move forward.

"So you won't be happy unless I pledge my undying love for you?" His sarcastic tone made the words come out like a scathing rebuke. Oliver saw her flinch and regretted speaking so harshly. "What about moving in with me? Or are you planning to reject that offer as well?"

She squared her shoulders and met his hostility with calm resolve. "With everything you have going on with your family and what's happening with your father, I'm not sure that's a great idea."

"You're turning me down because my father's in prison?"

"I'm turning you down," Sammi began in soothing tones, "because since he's come back, you're so angry about having to confront your past."

"So I'm angry at my father. That has nothing to do with you and me."

"Your bitterness toward your family dominates your emotions," she explained. "You told me you turned to drugs to escape feeling bad all the time. Yet resentment toward your brothers drives your ambition, and you avoid having anything to do with your mother unless it's absolutely necessary."

How could Oliver argue with her when everything she said was true? He was filled with hostility toward his family and convinced that if he cut off contact with them, he'd be happier. Only being apart from them didn't improve his mood. Past hurts continued to bother him like a wound that never healed, and he hated that he knew no way to fix the situation.

"So what do you suggest I do?" Oliver demanded, the weight of his sulky mood lowering his tone to a growl. Despite his rebellious attitude, he desperately wanted help.

"I think you should go see your father."

"In prison? Have you lost your mind? What possible good will that do except make him feel as if he's won?"

Sammi regarded him in dismay. "Won? This isn't a contest between you."

"Isn't it?" Oliver's throat closed down. When he forced out his next words, his voice held bleak resignation. "All I've ever done is fight for my father's recognition and approval. Nothing I ever did was good enough for him." Oliver rubbed his face. "Going to see him will only bring up all those bad feelings. I just want him out of my life."

"But he was out of your life, and I'm not sure it helped you."

This time the anger that flashed through Oliver was directed at her. How dare she comment on things she knew nothing about? Sure, when Vernon had first disappeared, Oliver let his rage drive him into destructive habits, but he pulled himself out of that nosedive. And once he'd realized he had nothing left to prove with his father gone, he'd been able to focus on being successful in a way that suited him.

No longer self-destructive with the need to fail and demonstrate that his father had been right all along, Oliver had capitalized on his talents and thrived. He threw his hand out, encompassing all that surrounded him.

"All you need to do is look at my achievements to realize that's not true."

"Yet you can't really say you're content."

"I've been happy with you," Oliver said, coming as close as he could to his ever-deepening feelings for her. "And I'm excited to be a father. Why can't you just agree to move in and be happy with me?"

"I really want that," Sammi admitted, her expression saying the opposite. "But all my life I've done things to please other people and let myself down. You've shown me how to be strong and stand up for what's good for me."

Oliver contemplated her meaning. "And you don't think I'm good for you."

"You are," she assured him. "But your anger isn't good for anyone."

"And you think going to see Vernon will solve everything."

"Not just seeing him," she offered in tentative tones, "but finding a way toward forgiving him. If you can't let go of your anger, you will always be its victim."

Being referred to as a victim made his irritation spike. Oliver ground his teeth to contain the savage rebuttal and asked, "How am I supposed to forgive him if he doesn't apologize? Because I'd be shocked if he takes responsibility for all he's done."

"Just because he hasn't had a change of heart doesn't mean you can't."

"Do you really expect me to forgive him for being a worthless human being? He didn't give a damn about any of us when he stole millions and ran off, abandoning my mother, my brothers and me to deal with the authorities and everyone he'd cheated. Everyone blamed us because he wasn't around to focus their anger on. It wasn't fair. He should've stuck by us, but he's a selfish bastard, incapable of thinking about anybody but himself."

A second before his rage spun out of control, Oliver became aware of Sammi's rising dismay and lapsed into silence. His chest heaved as he gulped in air. Over the last few minutes, his heightened emotional state illustrated why she didn't want to be with him. He was driving a wedge between them with his anger, and if he refused to deal with it, she might leave him.

"You're right," he admitted, shying away from his fear

of losing her. "I'm angry. But if you think going to visit my father in prison can help me deal with that, then you have no idea what I'm going through."

"What do you think about this?" Sammi asked, emerging from the dressing room in a strapless satin dress of bold chartreuse that popped against her dark hair.

Kimberly glanced away from her reflection and nodded. "I like it. What do you think about this?" She indicated the blue velvet jacket dress that showed off her mile-long legs and enhanced the blue of her eyes. "Strappy sandals or thigh-high boots?"

"Definitely the boots."

Sammi dropped her arm onto the other woman's shoulder, and the two of them adopted the broken lines and bored expressions of an editorial photoshoot. Behind them, several women watched in fascination.

The two models were out shopping for something to wear to a launch party later that night. Adina was introducing a new line of vegan leather purses at Into the Now, a SoHo boutique that featured luxury-brand sustainable fashion, makeup and accessories. Both Kimberly and Sammi had taken part in the media campaign that had preceded the launch and been invited to the opening.

Decisions made, both women made their purchases and headed to a nearby restaurant for lunch. Since Oliver's proposal two days before, Sammi had been eager to talk to her friend about it but preferred to have the discussion face-to-face.

"Something happened with Oliver the other day," Sammi said, digging into her salad with gusto.

Kimberly scrutinized her friend. "Something good or bad?"

"I'm not sure," Sammi admitted. "He asked me to marry him."

"Wow! That's fast."

"Too fast. I turned him down."

"How come?" Kimberly had been following Sammi's romantic journey with Oliver and knew all about her friend's hopes and fears surrounding the relationship. "I mean, you're crazy about the guy, and he's obviously into you."

"I've fallen hard for him, but I don't know if he'll ever feel the same way about me." Sammi released a shaky breath.

In the hours following Oliver's proposal, she'd been clearheaded and firm in her resolve. But the more time that passed, the more she waffled. Would marrying Oliver be such a bad thing? Even though he didn't love her, she knew he wouldn't cheat. He'd been clear about his disgust with his father over Vernon's numerous dalliances and the misery this had caused Oliver's mother. A man as strong in his beliefs as Oliver wouldn't go back on them, and even though that meant he had a hard time letting go of his anger, Sammi knew he would devote himself to their family. But was duty enough for her? If her physical passions were satisfied, but her heart remained empty, could she ever be happy?

"I want to believe he could come to love me," Sammi continued, "but I'm afraid that he's too pessimistic to let down his walls. It all goes back to how his father treated him as a kid. His older brothers got all the attention while Oliver was ignored and unappreciated. All he wanted was his father's love, and no matter what he did, how much he excelled in school or at sports, Josh and Jake were the sons their father praised." Sammi didn't blame Oliver for being skeptical when it came to putting his heart on display. "And now that his father is back, he's angry all the time."

"But it'll get better after the trial is over, won't it?"

"I don't know," Sammi admitted. "Because he can't let go of his resentment over how Vernon treated him growing up, his temper keeps him from trusting and opening his heart."

"Have you brought up counseling?" Kimberly asked.

"I haven't." But not because Oliver might be unwilling to talk about his feelings. He'd been in therapy while dealing his addiction. No, it was Sammi whose whole body went cold at the thought of discussing their issues. What if she received clear confirmation that their relationship was doomed? "He's been angry for so long… I'm not sure he wants to let go of it." The familiar darkness had become such a part of him that she worried he knew no other way to exist.

"So what are you going to do?"

"If I'm unwilling to raise my child in a negative environment, I need to make a decision about our relationship as soon as possible."

Later that evening, Sammi's conversation with Kimberly seemed like an overreaction as she emerged from Oliver's bedroom. His eyebrows went up as he took in her new finery, and Sammi trembled beneath the onslaught of appreciation radiating from him.

"You look incredible," he murmured, taking her hand and turning her slowly so he could admire her from every angle. "Absolutely gorgeous."

He wrapped his arm around her waist and kissed his way along her temple to her ear, where he began whispering provocative alternatives to that night's event. Sammi's skin flushed as he nibbled on her earlobe, but she set her hand on his chest and pushed him back with a breathless laugh.

"I really should put in an appearance." Her stomach tightened at his anguished groan, intensifying the lust that had awakened at his nearness. "After all, I was part of the campaign."

"Then later," he promised, twin flames lighting his blue eyes.

Even though Into the Now was only a few short blocks from Oliver's loft, the early November weather had turned blustery, so they grabbed a cab for the short trip.

In addition to many of Sammi's fellow models, the event was attended by several A-list actors, New York City socialites and fashion influencers. Sammi and Oliver circulated through the guests, chatting with those they knew. With Oliver's hand resting possessively on her hip, Sammi tried to relax. Things hadn't gone smoothly when they'd made their first public appearance over a week ago, and since then, the only time they seemed to connect was in bed. Not that she was complaining.

Although their polite interactions during the day left Sammi with an aching heart, at night they came together in frantic, explosive hunger that shattered her defenses and left her convinced that they'd figure out a way past their difficulties. Unfortunately, as the sun warmed the bedroom she and Oliver shared, the happy glow of their lovemaking faded. She'd venture to the kitchen for breakfast and find Oliver polite and solicitous, but firmly withdrawn behind a wall of mundane conversation.

They existed in a bubble where only the present mattered. Neither discussed the future, and the past only raised hurts that couldn't be healed. Oliver ceased all mention of the media blitz surrounding his father's upcoming trial, and the only time he brought up the baby was to ask how she was feeling. His care for her was apparent, but that was no match for his pessimism.

Yet tonight, as the evening progressed, Oliver demonstrated the sort of warm affection that left Sammi reevaluating her behavior. Were her doubts getting in the way of their deepening relationship? After all, she'd been the one who'd denied that they were a couple. Sammi recognized that her hesitation was driven by her fears. She was so determined to make wise decisions about their future that she was keeping him at arm's length.

They were chatting with Kimberly and her fiancé about his project that the two women had participated in when Oliver's phone began to buzz. He surreptitiously slipped it from his pocket and glanced at the screen.

"Vernon's lawyer," Oliver explained, answering her quizzical look.

"You can't keep dodging his calls," she advised, her enthusiasm for the event waning as Oliver's expression darkened. "If you're not going to visit your father, tell him."

With a grim nod, Oliver excused himself and headed off. Sammi remained behind and was chatting with her friends when Kimberly nudged her. Glancing in the direction her friend indicated, Sammi spied Ty with a leggy blonde on his arm. As if aware of her attention, Ty's gaze locked with hers. His glower was so fierce that Sammi knew he would make trouble if they crossed paths. Deciding she'd rather face him with Oliver beside her, Sammi excused herself and went in search of him.

Most of the action was happening on the first three levels of the six-floor boutique. She spotted him in a back hall on the third floor, just past the elevators.

Despite the party noise behind her, Sammi was able to hear Oliver's side of the conversation. His tense voice revealed his agitation.

"I don't give a damn what my father wants. I'm not going to visit him. Ever."

Sammi retreated before she was caught spying and fled back toward the party. Overhearing Oliver's side of the

conversation with Vernon Lowell's lawyer gave Sammi a
lot to think about. The level of rage Oliver felt toward his
father made her anxious. While Sammi was growing up,
her mother had often demonstrated the same sort of turbulent outbursts whenever something surrounding Sammi's
career had gone awry. She understood now that the anger
had been born of fear, that Celeste was terrified of falling
back into the poverty she'd known as a child.

Sammi craved the sort of emotional stability she'd
never known growing up, and if Oliver's virulent outbursts
weren't healthy for her to be around, then she certainly
didn't want her child drinking in all the negativity that
the drama unfolding with his family incited. What made
it worse was how he'd shut her out while dwelling on all
the things that had gone wrong in the past. How could she
plan a future with him when he refused to let her be a full
partner in his present?

So had she just decided against moving in? Was it really
that cut-and-dried? Or should she ask Oliver to join her in
counseling to work on his anger issues? She'd been around
him long enough to know that he could keep a promise.
He'd been sober for eight years. And he was maintaining his
sobriety despite the upheaval of his father's upcoming trial.

On her way toward the elegant stairs that divided the
narrow boutique into exclusive shopping opportunities,
Sammi was too lost in thought to pay attention to her surroundings.

"I thought you might be here" came a smug masculine
voice.

Sammi stopped as she realized her way was blocked by
her ex. "Hello, Ty," she said, noting his immaculate navy
suit and crisp white shirt. "Sorry I can't stay and chat, but
my friend is looking for me."

The excuse sounded lame, but she had no interest in

engaging with Ty. She made to brush past him, but Ty reached out and stopped her. To Sammi's surprise, she felt no inclination to cringe away from the malice narrowing her ex-boyfriend's eyes.

"Let go of me," she warned, twisting her arm free from the cruel bite of his fingers.

"You mean that guy you're with? Oliver Lowell, right?"

"Yes…" Sammi drew out the affirmation, wondering why Ty was looking so sly.

"So," her ex muttered ominously, "you were behind it."

"Behind what?" Sammi squared her shoulders and looked Ty straight in the eye, seeing the insecurity that made him behave like a bully. Why hadn't she realized what he was long ago and saved herself a whole lot of misery?

"Like you don't know," Ty sneered. "I lost my job thanks to you."

"Thanks to me? I have no idea what you're talking about. And I certainly didn't have anything to do with you losing your job."

"Your denial might be more believable if you weren't here with Lowell."

"What does that have to do with anything?"

"Fine. Play the innocent," he sniffed. "A couple weeks after you and I broke up, my manager sits me down, tells me there's been a series of complaints about me from my biggest client."

If he treated them with the same disdain he'd shown her, then Sammi wasn't surprised he'd gotten into trouble.

"What does any of that have to do with Oliver or me?"

"It took me a while to connect the dots, but eventually I found out that the person stirring up trouble was your date."

"Oliver?" she breathed, suddenly feeling sick. "That makes no sense. Why would he go out of his way to make trouble for you?"

"At the time I had no idea. In fact, none of it made any sense until I saw the two of you together tonight."

"What are you saying?"

"That you asked him to mess with me."

"What? That's absurd."

"Is it? You two look pretty cozy. How long have you known each other?"

Sammi stared at her ex-boyfriend in puzzlement. "We met in September."

"When in September?"

Sammi tossed her head. "If you have to know, the night we broke up."

"And you've been going out this whole time?"

"No, I was in Paris for fashion week and didn't see him again until early October. Why?"

"So when you two met that night, you didn't cry on his shoulder about how I'd dumped you?" He paused and leered. "Or why?"

"I didn't." Sammi frowned, trying to recall that evening and what they'd talked about. "I mean he asked me if I was okay. He'd obviously seen what happened between us before you took off. And stuck me with the unpaid bar tab," she added in a spiteful afterthought.

"So you wanted a little revenge."

Sammi frowned, trying to wrap her head around what he was saying. "That's not true. And besides, Oliver has no idea who you are. How could he possibly cause you to lose your job?"

"We met that night as I was leaving. He dumped a drink on me, and I gave him my business card so he could pay for my dry cleaning."

"I'm sure it's all a big coincidence."

"Some coincidence when I see you two looking all lovey-dovey," Ty said in a dark tone. "You can deny it all you want, but I know you were behind the whole thing."

Sammi reeled as Ty's accusation struck her. "I knew nothing about any of this," she declared, wishing she could speak for Oliver, as well. "And I'm sure if your client complained about you, there was a reason for it." Sammi didn't wait for Ty to reply before heading back the way she'd come. Toward Oliver.

Was it possible that he'd done something so devious and harmful to Ty? And for what purpose? For her? Had she said something that spurred Oliver to act? Or had his anger gotten the better of him?

Sick to her stomach, she ducked into a restroom and leaned heavily on the counter until her breathing slowed. Ty's accusation spun through her head, pinning her in place. What was she supposed to do with what she'd learned? Her phone buzzed with a text. She glanced at the screen and saw that Oliver was looking for her. The idea of confronting him about what Ty said filled her with dread, but what if she told him about her encounter with Ty and Oliver did something even worse?

Sammi knew she'd never be able to keep silent. She wanted an honest relationship with Oliver, both for herself and her child. And if that meant she had to give up on the idea of being a couple with him... She'd already given him her heart. The thought of wrenching it away made her ache. Oliver would always be a part of her life. But he had to know that his anger issues were posed to do all of them harm.

Decision made, she texted Oliver back, letting him know that she wasn't feeling well and would meet him near the entrance. Then, bracing herself for the conversation to come, she headed for the elevator.

Eleven

In the quiet back corridor on the boutique's third floor, Oliver hung up on his father's lawyer and stewed. How could Vernon possibly believe he deserved forgiveness or redemption or whatever the hell he thought he might achieve by seeing his sons? Oliver was only too happy to disappoint him.

He knew Sammi was waiting, no doubt worried how the call had gone, but the anger surging through his veins needed to die down before he faced her. Tonight's event was all about her, and he'd spoil the mood if he stormed back filled with irritation.

It was getting harder each day to moderate his temper around her. Everywhere he turned, he was forced to contend with people's curiosity about his father's upcoming trial. Nonstop leaks spilled tidbits involving the evidence that had been gathered; New York newspapers wrote articles featuring the families who'd lost everything to Vernon Lowell's larceny. Oliver couldn't go anywhere without confronting his father's wrongdoing.

The deluge threw salt in unhealed wounds, and with each day that passed Oliver struggled to stay sober. He'd started attending meetings again, finding comfort in anonymity. Yet although the community helped him, he hadn't shared with Sammi that he was going. He was trying to convince her to move in with him and didn't want his struggles to create an obstacle to that.

Finally calmer, Oliver went back downstairs to find Sammi. He sent her a text asking her location. Passing one of the bars set up on each level, he paused. As much as he loved the burn of whiskey as it blazed its way down his throat, he appreciated its numbing qualities just as much. The urge to toss down several shots of whatever decent vintage the bartender had on hand nearly overwhelmed him before Oliver got his feet moving again.

If merely contemplating a meeting with his father left him grappling with the addiction that had nearly killed him, Oliver knew he'd been right to reject all pressure to visit Vernon in prison. He paused near the second-floor landing as his phone buzzed, indicating he'd received a text. Sammi. He quickly scanned her text, concern rushing through him at her message.

Did her sudden illness mean something was wrong with the baby or was it merely normal sickness brought about by her pregnancy? Oliver rushed down the remaining stairs, and when he didn't see Sammi anywhere inside the entrance, he moved through the door and onto the SoHo street.

Relief struck him as he spied her off to one side, her slim body wrapped in her long wool coat with faux fur accents. The welcome sight of her, shivering in the chilly night air, smothered the last of his bad temper as he approached her.

"Are you okay?"

"I'm fine." She took the arm he offered and drew him

toward the curb. "I just need some fresh air. Let's go back to your place."

Remembering all the pleasurable activities he'd promised her earlier, Oliver hailed a cab and slid in beside her. Although she claimed to be feeling better, Oliver noted something remained off with her. He scanned her profile and noticed the rigid quality of her expression. Was she still feeling sick and didn't want to worry him? He squeezed her hand in a reassuring manner, and her gaze barely softened as it flicked toward him.

"Did something happen at the party?" he asked as they entered his building and moved toward his elevator.

"I ran into Ty." She leaned her back against the elevator wall, and her watchful gaze took in his reaction.

For a moment he had a hard time placing the name, and then he remembered its significance. "Your ex. Did he say something to upset you?"

"You might say that."

The floor shifted as the elevator stopped, disrupting his balance. The doors opened, and he watched as Sammi stepped into the hallway that led to his apartment. Oliver followed, recalling his aversion to the way Ty had treated her that night. And what he had done about it.

"You should've told me earlier," he said smoothly, keying the code that unlocked his door. The tension she'd displayed in the taxi seemed more tangible now, something she'd placed between them to keep him away. "I would've had a chat with him."

"I think you've already done enough." Sammi walked upstairs and stopped in the middle of his living room and spun around to confront him. "He said you were responsible for him losing his job. Is that true?"

"I had a conversation with a friend of mine," Oliver admitted, his gut twisting as disappointment flashed across her beautiful face. He recognized the sensation. It happened every time his father's critical gaze landed on him. He flinched away from the emotions crawling through him.

Sammi rolled her lips between her teeth and stared at him for several heartbeats. "Did you know it would lead to him getting fired? Did you mean for that to happen?"

"Yes. The man is a bully who picked on a woman he was dating. He picked on you. You can't expect that I wouldn't defend you."

"But you didn't defend me," she argued, wrapping her arms around her middle. "And you didn't do it for me. You got mad and took revenge because you were angry. He said it happened in September." Between accusations, her breath came in unsteady rasps. "You didn't even know me."

He thought about the night they'd spent together and its effect on him.

I did know you.

"Regardless," he said, the anger he'd tamped down earlier rising to meet her outrage. All Oliver had wanted to do was make things right for her, and this was the thanks he got? "You didn't deserve to be treated like that. He needed to get a taste of his own medicine."

"Maybe, but it wasn't your decision to make. He hurt *me*." She jabbed her finger into her chest. "And I could choose whether to retaliate or forgive."

"And what did you choose?" he asked, already knowing she'd never retaliate. He recalled her naive suggestion that he forgive his father. Just the thought of it burned Oliver's patience to a blackened crisp. Vernon didn't deserve sympathy or compassion, and Oliver would be damned if he'd give him forgiveness.

"Once I met you," Sammi said, her soft voice aching with sadness. "I had no need to do either. You entered my world and all I could think about was being with you. Everything else faded away. It was as if my life started the day we met."

Oliver had no words. He realized that he felt the exact same way. That was why he'd been so focused on finding her. And now she was leaving him once more.

"I didn't mean to upset you," he said.

"I know. I guess what I feel is disappointment. I thought your anger was something that hurt only you because it makes you isolate yourself from everyone around you."

Despite her calm, measured tone, her words lashed at him. He hated being called out for doing something he believed in. And disappointing her reminded him too much of how he felt as a kid. As if nothing he did was good enough.

"Until now," she continued, "I didn't realize that your anger makes you want to hurt others. And that scares me. I'm afraid for what you do next. Who you'll hurt next. I'm afraid it will be me."

Her assertion landed on him like a concrete wall.

"I'd never do anything to hurt you."

"Maybe not intentionally, but Ty thinks I encouraged you to go after him. He thinks it's my fault that he got fired, and if he spreads that around, that could ruin my reputation and any chance I have of making a profitable pivot in my career."

Oliver shook his head, rejecting her concerns. "You don't need to worry. I'll take care of you."

Her eyes widened. "I don't want you to take care of me. I want you to recognize that I'm capable and have my back. I don't need you to do battle for me. I want you to cheer me on."

"And you know I do."

"How?" Her breath grew shaky even as her voice gained strength. "By talking me out of moving into an apartment I can afford? And constantly telling me I don't have to worry about money because you'll take care of me and the baby?"

"If you want me to help you find an apartment that you can afford, I will." The words pained him to say, but she obviously needed him to say them.

"Good, because I don't plan on moving in with you." She looked more determined than he'd ever seen her. "Or marrying you."

Didn't she understand what it meant that he'd proposed? It wasn't just for convenience's sake. They were going to have a baby together. He wanted them to grow closer. But while the power of their physical chemistry couldn't be denied, they both remained barricaded behind walls, unwilling to risk being hurt.

"Not ever?" he demanded, panic making it impossible for him to think clearly. "Or not now? If you need time, I get it. We've been moving fast, but I don't want to lose you. I can't lose you."

"Let's go down to your studio," she said, the change of topic catching him off guard.

"Why?"

She headed for the stairs that led below. "I want you to take the picture of me you promised that first night. I paid for it. I want you to take it."

He'd made the offer in a bid to get to know her better, but she'd obviously taken the transaction more seriously. "Why now?"

"For weeks now I've had it in my head that once you take the picture, you'll lose interest in me because in the process you'll know all my secrets." She glanced at him over her shoulder. "I guess the time has come for me to face that fear."

He trailed after her down the stairs while protests spun through his mind. He longed to assure her that he'd never let her go. She was as necessary to him as the air he breathed, but he'd glimpsed resistance in her somber expression.

Words between them weren't enough for her to believe him. She needed proof.

"You don't trust me," he breathed.

Sammi reached the bottom and faced him without speaking. He could see the answer in her eyes. She needed him to do better. To stop being angry. But he didn't know how. The rage had been with him for so long that it affected him on a cellular level. He couldn't just wish it away even if he wanted to.

"I can't take the photo tonight," he said, troubled by all she was asking of him.

"You've done all the real work already," she reminded him. Reaching the studio, she picked up one of his cameras and brought it to him. "You've asked all the questions and dug deep into my psyche. The only thing that's left is to take the photo that will reveal it all."

He crossed his arms and refused to accept the camera. He feared with her mind made up, if he did as she asked, she would then use the photo session to justify leaving him.

"You're crazy if you think a single photo session is all it will take for me to lose interest in you."

She pushed the camera hard into his chest. "Take the picture and let's see."

Dizzy with apprehension, Sammi watched as her words hit their mark. What was she doing? Did she really want to lose Oliver with her ultimatum? Her declaration had been a gauntlet thrown at his feet. She was daring him to end things between them and risking that he'd let his stubborn anger rule him.

With her trembling fingers barely able to maintain the grip on the camera she'd thrust against his chest, Sammi withstood the onslaught of Oliver's heated stare. With each second that passed, he grew more rigid and more resistant, and her hopes failed. If he'd been a castle, the portcullis had just slammed shut, leaving her outside in the cold.

She'd pushed him too far. She could see it in his shuttered expression. In the abrupt way he plucked the camera from her grasp. By confessing her fear, she'd revealed her faith in him was failing. Her eyes burned as tears threatened. Maybe she could still take it all back, agree to marry him on his terms. Being with him was better than cutting him out of her life. She loved him enough for both of them.

And then she recalled what Oliver had done to Ty on her behalf.

Could she really let him drown in his bitterness and regrets, or was she going to challenge him to do better? Loving him meant she had to be brave enough to goad him into fighting for their future and, failing that, be willing to let him go.

"Fine," he said. "Let's do this."

Nodding, Sammi stripped out of her coat and let it fall over a nearby table. Next, she crossed to the makeup table and used makeup remover to strip away her carefully applied mask. Slipping out of her dress, she wrapped her body in a robe. Whatever came next, she intended to be raw and open to it.

She'd been photographed by hundreds of photographers and recognized that Oliver's talent far exceeded anyone else's she knew. Her heartbeat quickened as she imagined what it would be like to pose for him. Only this wouldn't be an ordinary photoshoot. So much was changing in his world. Between her pregnancy and his father's upcoming trial, Oliver was under a great deal of pressure. He coped by throwing himself into work, escaping into something he could control.

While she'd cleaned her face and scraped her hair back into a messy bun, Oliver had adjusted the lighting and brought a stool into the middle of the white backdrop.

She crossed the bleak landscape and settled onto the seat, breathing deep to relax her muscles and free herself from tension.

"Tell me something you've always wanted to do but haven't," Oliver began, his tone warmer than she expected, inviting her to share confidences.

Sammi thought about all the conversations they'd had and what she hadn't told him about herself. While he waited in silent stillness, she considered and discarded a dozen inconsequential things before settling on something she'd avoided.

"I've never gone to the Philippines to visit." Sammi spoke the words quietly. "And I have family there that I'll never get to meet."

"Why is that?"

"Until I was ten, I had it in my head that there was a perfect family awaiting me on the other side of the world if only we had enough money to go visit them. But that wasn't the case. My mom grew up dirt-poor. Her father died when she was five, and her mother had to work in the fields. She could barely make enough to feed them, much less keep a roof over their heads. When my mom was eleven, they moved to the city where my grandmother's sister lived, and my grandmother got a job as a maid in a rich man's house."

Sammi paused to let Oliver absorb where she'd come from and wondered if that changed his perception of her. His mother had come from old money and grew up in the sort of house where Sammi's grandmother had worked.

"Things improved somewhat for my mother after that. My grandmother was able to afford a studio apartment and send my mom to school. Neither one of my grandparents had anything beyond an elementary-level education, and my mother knew the only way to improve her life was through schooling."

"Do you know if your grandmother is still alive?"

Sammi shrugged. "I have no idea or how to find out."

"What about your father?"

"When my mom met him, he was already married." Sammi noticed Oliver's grim expression and shook her head. "She didn't know until after she got pregnant."

"Is that when she came to the US?"

"My father's father-in-law paid her way here and made her promise never to contact my father again." Sammi's heart ached as she remembered the broken tears in her mother's eyes the night she'd told the story. "He didn't want his daughter to learn of her husband's infidelity. Or for there to be an illegitimate child who might one day make trouble."

"So you were her ticket out," Oliver murmured.

"I guess I was." Before her mother had revealed her assumption that Sammi would terminate her pregnancy, she'd always believed that Celeste had wanted to be a mother. Now she had a different perspective and still hadn't figured out how to cope with this new reality. "I really don't know if she wanted me."

"Did you ever ask?"

"Until recently it never occurred to me that I had to."

"That has to make you angry at your mother."

"Of course." Sammi sighed. "But it's a little less every day. For a long time I resented the pressure she put on me to model and make money. Facing the loss of my income because I'm pregnant has given me a new perspective. I'm starting to appreciate how terrified she was of being poor again. I can't blame her for doing whatever she needed to survive."

"I suppose next you're going to tell me you've forgiven her."

Sammi heard the resentment beneath Oliver's skepticism. "I need to let go of my resentment because it's not doing me or my mother any good. I'm as angry with myself for not trusting my instincts and letting her run my life as I am angry with her for using me all these years."

"The difference between us is that I'm not angry with myself," Oliver pointed out. "I'm angry with my father."

Sammi thought of her tumultuous relationship with her mother and knew that it wasn't that simple. "The difference between us is that I recognize she's the only family I have and I won't be happy if she's not in my life. I've decided to put the past behind me. We're having lunch tomorrow to celebrate her new job. Hopefully it'll be a fresh start for both of us."

As she finished talking, Oliver walked over and set his camera on a nearby table.

"Is that it?" she asked, getting to her feet. "Did you get the shot?"

"I don't know." His gaze was fixed at a point behind her. "I took a lot of photos."

"I thought we agreed that I would pay you to take one."

"I realized that a single shot can't capture who you are." Oliver shifted his attention and looked directly at her. "I was wrong to think that it could."

Sammi's throat seized up, preventing her from speaking. Instead, she led Oliver to the couch, stripped him out of his clothes and took him into her mouth. Kneeling between his strong thighs, she blocked every thought from her mind and channeled each painful thump of her heart into pleasuring him. Gripping his shaft, she caressed the head while swirling her tongue along his velvet length. His sharp exhalation made her smile. His tortured breaths filled her ears as she worked over him with tongue, lips and hand. She knew he was close when he began bucking into her mouth.

"Stop!" He growled the word. Snagging fingers in her long hair, he tugged her head back. "Not like this. I need to be inside you."

With an economy of movement, Sammi stripped off her robe and underwear. His hands reached for her as she straddled his lap. She tossed her hair away from her face and braced her hands on his shoulders.

"Like this?" Slowly she lowered herself, letting his erection impale her.

"Yes." His voice was a hoarse whisper as his fingers bit into her hips.

She began to move, half on her own, half directed by him. Wild emotions burst free as she rode his shaft, pumping as he thrust into her. For this moment she was his to own, to command. Every flex of his hard muscles sent her hard and fast into her building pleasure. Unable to look away as he threw back his head and closed his eyes, she watched a flush stain his cheeks. The heat beneath his skin burned into her flesh, sending sensation rushing through her.

Desire built. Passion grew in intensity. She panted as her inner muscles clenched and pulled him deeper. Each time they made love she experienced such intense physical pleasure, but this time, opening her heart and giving him everything, transcended anything she'd ever known.

Sammi cried out as her orgasm slammed into her like a tsunami. She clung to Oliver as the powerful wave wiped out everything in its path. Her fear and anxiety shattered. Resentment and blame swept away and were gone, leaving behind the scoured sand upon which she would build her new life.

Oliver's arms came around her, holding her secure as his climax arrived like a storm. His shudders made her chest ache. Had he too been unmade by the power of their passion? Was he ready to create something new on the ashes of past hurts and grief?

Or did he remain unwilling to give up the familiar patterns that kept him from growing? And how could she move forward with him if that was the case?

Twelve

The morning following the party at Into the Now, Oliver woke alone in bed for the first time in weeks. Groggy from lack of sleep, he lay still and listened, ears straining for any sound of movement in the apartment. The absolute quiet stirred his alarm.

She could've just gotten up and made coffee. Her absence from the bed didn't mean she was gone. Nor did her early departure mean she wasn't coming back.

As angry and disappointed as she'd been, would she have made love with him if it was over? Still, the desperation in her kisses and the fierce emotion she'd displayed was new. It was as if she'd been trying to cling to something, knowing it was already gone. And at the peak of their frantic coupling, he could swear he'd seen something break in her eyes. Something that set off a chain reaction of despair and sorrow in him. She'd been so calm in the aftermath, so steady and sure. A woman who knew what she wanted and intended to get it. What eluded him was knowing if what she wanted was him.

Oliver rolled out of bed and headed for the closet. He cataloged her clothes with a quick glance and decided she hadn't moved out. His relief was short-lived, however, because when he walked into the bathroom, he noted that the familiar collection of creams and makeup she used on a daily basis was gone.

He headed back to his nightstand but saw no sign of his phone. Flashing to the night before, he realized it was still downstairs with his discarded clothes. After a quick glance at the clock, he determined it was too late in the morning for him to risk wandering around naked, so he slid into a pair of boxer briefs and headed to his studio.

Heidi had the coffee on when he arrived. His clothes sat in a neat pile on the bottom step along with Sammi's sexy black underwear.

"Hey," he said to his assistant, digging through the jacket pockets and unearthing his phone. "Do we have anything going today?"

"No meetings or shoots, if that's what you're asking about."

"Great."

He opened his text app, preparing to send a message to Sammi, and paused. What could he say to her that he hadn't already shared in bed last night? The problems that existed between them couldn't be fixed with great sex. Not only had he failed to give her the love she needed, but he'd also broken her trust with the stunt he'd pulled on her ex-boyfriend.

"I was wondering if you could do me a favor," he said, accepting the mug of coffee Heidi brought over.

"You pay me to do all kinds of favors for you," his assistant said with a wry smile that faded as she noticed his expression. "Whatever you need."

"Send two dozen red roses to…" He trailed off, realizing he couldn't fix what was wrong with the romantic gesture. The only way forward with her was through letting go of his resentment toward his family and especially his father. "Scratch that," he amended, determined to do something nice for one of the women in his life. "Take the day off. Use the corporate card and go get yourself a pedicure or take a friend to lunch. Or do both. Or neither. Just do something nice for yourself, on me."

Heidi's eyes had widened with shock as he'd spoken. "Are you sure? What if somebody calls?"

"Then we will call them back tomorrow. Go have fun."

Leaving his stunned assistant staring after him in confusion, Oliver headed upstairs. He opened the app, pulled up his recent calls and dialed the one at the top. When he reached his father's lawyer, Oliver made arrangements to visit Vernon in prison.

He didn't need a series of empty days and nights without Sammi to wake him up. He'd already spent too much time letting his anger and hurt isolate him from the people he loved. In his heart, he knew that she'd been right. Confronting his father was the key to dealing with the anger that plagued him. As long as he avoided the source of his pain, he would never overcome the fear of rejection that was separating him from Sammi.

Three hours later, Oliver was on his way to the federal prison that housed his father. He'd been surprised how swiftly the visit had been arranged and somewhat relieved. Less time to second-guess his decision would avoid the chance that he'd back out.

Dismal gray walls closed in on Oliver as he headed into the heart of the facility. Anxiety, tension and anger mixed in his gut as he readied himself to see his father for the first time in a decade and a half. Bile rose, and he clenched his teeth to keep it down. As he went through the visitor procedures, Oliver wondered what the hell he was doing. How could anything good come out of seeing a father he despised? Especially when he knew Vernon had never loved him. What would Oliver gain by acknowledging that his father continued to sway his emotions?

Sammi believed that Vernon's disappearance left Oliver with unresolved issues. He might resist acknowledging it, but every time he reflected on his childhood, he burned with outrage. As a kid he'd longed for his dad's approval. Yet no matter how he strove to stand out, his efforts failed. Thanks to his father's constant criticism, by the time he hit his teenage years, Oliver had stopped trying to please his father and acted out instead. Yet unlike Jake, who'd seemed to enjoy being a troublemaker, Oliver's bad behavior had been a cry for attention. A cry that had been ignored.

Ignored. Isolated. Unloved.

Was it at all surprising that Oliver had sought to numb himself with drugs and alcohol? And as much as he regretted the years of addiction, Oliver had escaped the downward spiral on his own. No one in his family had reached out a helping hand. No, Oliver had done that all on his own. He'd dug himself out of his pit of despair. He'd given up drugs. He'd gotten himself clean. No one had helped. Just like he'd been successful because of his drive and his talent and his determination. Oliver had become a success, not because of his father, but in spite of his father. He'd succeeded because of the mistakes he'd made and what he learned from them.

With his heart pounding in his throat hard enough to choke him, Oliver entered a long room partitioned into visitor and inmate spaces. He hadn't known exactly what to expect when he'd come to the prison, but he was relieved that he wouldn't be alone with his father or face-to-face with open space between them. This setting, with the clear glass defining who was the visitor and who was the criminal, eased Oliver's discomfort somewhat. He joined the half a dozen people engaged in conversations, selecting an empty seat, when he realized Vernon hadn't yet arrived.

Dropping onto the smooth plastic chair, he noticed the low rumbling discomfort was growing louder, like a freight train coming at him from a distant place. The sensation had been building in him since Sammi had suggested he confront his past. Now a tremor went through him as childhood fear and anxiety escalated, crippling his self-confidence. Suddenly he was no longer a successful photographer with his pick of assignments, but a miserable little boy who'd craved his father's attention, knowing he would never get it. For years Oliver had used drugs and alcohol to repress that scared child, but denying him kept him from healing.

Then Sammi had come along, her love and friendship chipping away at his defenses. Lulled by a sense of belonging, he stopped bracing against rejection and surrendered to a connection that felt so amazing, it terrified him. With Sammi he wanted to do better, be better. What he lacked was the confidence that he could succeed. No surprise then that his fear led him to behave badly.

The door leading into the prisoner's side opened, drawing Oliver's attention to the new arrival. A shock traveled through Oliver as he studied the man who approached. Despite his fit frame and the lack of gray hair, Vernon looked older. A network of wrinkles had been etched into his tan skin from a decade and a half in the sun. What had he been doing? No doubt fishing, Oliver thought, remembering the equipment he received from an anonymous source. Except for the dark circles beneath his eyes and the prison uniform he wore, Vernon Lowell looked as if he'd just returned from a long, relaxing vacation.

Well, he was back in the real world now, and his demeanor reflected that he knew it. The swagger that had once made his father seem all-powerful had been dimmed by his time behind bars. Yet some arrogance remained in the directness of his gaze as he sneered at his fellow inmates.

It was this confidence and his father's hypocrisy that sparked Oliver's temper. A second later, his anger flared to life as Vernon's eyes narrowed when he spied who awaited him. No doubt his father was disappointed that Oliver was the son who had been the first to visit. Vernon had never had time for his youngest son before. Oliver expected his father was most curious about Josh and Jake and would be eager to hear how Black Crescent had been reborn beneath his eldest son's leadership.

As Vernon sat down on the opposite side of the partition, he flashed his white teeth in a mocking grin. All of Oliver's muscles locked up in response. He couldn't move. He could only stare at his father and hate. This wasn't some joyful reunion. His father had no right to happiness. For fifteen years Oliver's mother had suffered from being abandoned by her husband and faced the anger and spite of the neighbors and friends whom he'd cheated. She defended him at first, foolishly trusting the man she'd married, believing that he wasn't responsible for their stolen fortunes. Oliver's heart ached for her.

Vernon picked up the phone and put it to his ear. His father's grin was sculpted in wax as he waited for Oliver to do the same so they could communicate. All the questions that had overwhelmed his mind on the trip here coalesced into one burning question. Vernon had once enjoyed everything that would've satisfied even the greediest of men. Yet he'd left it all behind and disappeared without a trace.

Were they all so disposable in his eyes that he'd let his wife and sons believe he was dead this whole time?

Moving as if through mud, Oliver picked up the phone and put it to his ear. He stared at his father, unwilling to begin the conversation.

"You look good," his father said, as if this was a normal conversation in a normal place on a normal day.

"So do you," Oliver retorted, his tone dripping with sardonic irony. "But then you've been on a tropical island these fifteen years, living the good life while the rest of us have been dealing with the aftermath of your mess."

"Your mother came by to visit," Vernon said, acting like he didn't hear his son's accusation or the venom in Oliver's tone. "Eve tells me you're a photographer. You always did like to mess around with that sort of stuff instead of focusing on important things."

Oliver hadn't come here to exchange fruitless barbs with this man. He'd come here for answers, and he intended to get some. But first he wanted to let Vernon know that he shouldn't expect they'd welcome his return with open arms.

"Do you know what disappearing with all that money did to your wife? Your family? Do you even care how much damage you've done?"

"I earned that money," Vernon asserted, his forehead puckering. "That was all money that I made because of what I could do."

Oliver gaped while his father rationalized the theft of millions of dollars, not just from clients who'd trusted him, but from his close friends. What kind of madness had possessed him to think that Vernon would take responsibility for all the harm he'd done? Putting aside his father's pathetic attempt to justify the theft, Oliver tried again.

"Why didn't you let any of us know that you were still alive?"

"I did." Vernon smirked. "I sent you a fishing rod. Didn't you get it?"

"I got it. Years too late." As Oliver spoke, he waited for the hot rage that always blindsided him, but all he felt was cool disdain. "What I don't understand is why you sent it."

Even as he asked, Oliver wondered why he was even bothering. Nothing Vernon said could fix what was wrong with Oliver. What the hell was he hoping to achieve with this visit? Even if Vernon made an effort, something the selfish bastard would never do, nothing his father could say would make up for the harm he'd caused a decade and a half earlier or his neglect during the years before that. For too long, Oliver had been waiting for something that Vernon couldn't possibly give him: peace.

How had he been so foolish to look for that outside himself? To give that much power to his father after everything that Vernon had done?

And then all the bad memories and debilitating doubts vanished in a flash of insight. Brightness exploded inside him, banishing the dark, bathing him in blessed relief.

He didn't need Vernon's answers. Didn't need his approval or his love. The only people Oliver needed for true happiness were Sammi and their baby. With her he could make a fresh start. Because of her he could release his anger and embrace a future where he reconnected with his brothers and his mom.

Almost giddy with relief, he hung up the phone and stood. If Vernon was surprised at his son's actions, Oliver never knew, because he didn't even glance at his father before turning and walking toward the exit.

A sense of lightness and calm filled him so he felt as if he were walking on a trampoline rather than the hard tile floor of the prison corridor. With each step he shed more and more of the weight that had hampered his spirit all these years. Reaching the outside, he lifted his face to the overcast sky and laughed as snow fell gently onto his skin. Overwhelmed by the sudden and intense need to see Sammi and tell her of today's insights, Oliver jogged toward the street.

"Congratulations!" Sammi lifted her sparkling water and clinked glasses with her mother. "The Paulson Agency is lucky to have you."

Sammi pondered the ripple effect of her collision with Oliver two months earlier. Not only had changes come to her and Oliver, but to her mother and Ty, as well. Would the ripple spread to Oliver's family next? If so, would it improve or further damage those relationships?

"I didn't realize how much I missed those days with you, taking you to photo shoots and go-sees, until I walked into Paulson."

Celeste's wistful smile transported Sammi back in time to those magical days when she and her mother rambled all over New York City. In those days she'd never glimpsed the stress her mother must've been under. Now she wondered if that had been because Celeste had enjoyed the long hours of travel, auditions, hair and makeup sessions, and photo shoots. In the days before Sammi booked her first major runway, it had been the two of them against the world. Once Sammi's career had taken off, her mother had been relegated to a lesser role.

"I'm sorry," Sammi said, her throat tight with regret.

Celeste looked surprised by the suddenly somber turn the conversation had taken. "Sorry for what?"

"I haven't said thank you for everything you've done for me."

Her mother blinked. "You don't need to thank me. It's a mother's job to take care of her child." Her genuine smile made Sammi's eyes water. "Even when her daughter doesn't need her anymore."

"I'll never not need you," Sammi said, her hand drifting over her abdomen. "Especially now. I need you more than ever."

"That's a relief," Celeste said. "After how things have been between us these last few weeks, I thought for sure you would cut me out of your life—"

Sammi interrupted. "You told me to terminate my pregnancy."

"That was the absolute wrong thing to say. I was thinking of your career, and mine, instead of considering how you felt and what you wanted." Celeste's expression twisted with regret. "I was afraid for you. I'm so sorry."

Although her heartache eased at her mother's apology, Sammi had been brooding over an important question for weeks. "Something has been bothering me since that day," Sammi admitted. "Do you regret having me?"

"No. Of course not." Celeste saw her daughter's skepticism and shrugged. "Maybe in the early days my life would've been easier for me if I hadn't become a mother at such a young age, but although I was terrified when I first learned I was pregnant, nothing in the world could have made me give you up."

The earnestness of her mother's confession gave Sammi hope that they could find their way back to the mother-daughter relationship she remembered from before her career took off.

"I can't imagine what it was like for you to leave behind everyone and everything you knew and move halfway around the world."

"I knew it would be a better life here." Celeste squeezed her daughter's hand. "I wanted a chance for a new beginning, and you're right, it wasn't easy. I had no skills and a high school education. I only hoped I could create a better life for you here than what I'd known in the Philippines."

"And you did," Sammi assured her. "If it wasn't for you, I wouldn't be the woman I am."

"And that woman is amazing," Celeste said, her eyes shining with pride. "You are strong and beautiful. And you are going to be a wonderful mother."

"I'm going to try to do as well as I can," Sammi said. "You've taught me a lot about sacrifice, and I hope my child appreciates me as much as I do you."

Her mother smiled a bit sadly. "That certainly is a change from how you felt about me these last few years."

"I guess I just needed a little space from you to put my life in perspective and understand all that you've done for me. In any given moment as I grew up I wanted to be with you and independent from you. There were times when I loved you and some when you were the last person I wanted to see. You know." Sammi grinned. "Normal mother-daughter-relationship stuff."

After lunch, Sammi returned to her apartment to pack the last few boxes and fill the suitcases she'd be taking with her to the studio apartment she'd rented. She was giving her apartment up the next day and needed someplace to go.

Even before learning last night what Oliver had done to Ty, she'd been leaning toward finding her own place. It had been his lack of remorse over how he let his anger dictate his actions that had put her mind at rest. The way things stood between them, moving in with Oliver was the wrong decision. Even though she loved him, even though she believed in his dream of cohabitating and co-parenting their child, when she'd gone all in and offered him her heart, he hadn't accepted it.

Nor was she surprised. As great as the sex was between them, Oliver had never given her any indication that he wanted to be in love. Rejection loomed too large in his mind for him to give himself over to her support. His lack of faith in them as a couple was an obstacle she couldn't overcome alone. Because of that, she'd decided to do what was best for her. She'd been in relationships before and knew when it wasn't working. This time was different, though. This time she'd wanted it to work, and it broke her heart that they could never be.

Thirteen

As the cab headed to Sammi's apartment through the gently drifting traffic-snarling snowflakes, Oliver had plenty of time to sort through the emotions that had gotten in the way of telling her how he felt about her. Instead of being honest with himself and her, he'd denied his growing feelings and marginalized their connection by denying her the closeness and intimate commitment she craved.

So how did he go about convincing her that he had changed overnight? After everything he'd put her through, would she believe that he'd let go of the past and was ready to have a future with her? Yet what could he say that might convince her when he demonstrated over and over that he was ruled by his anger?

Maybe he didn't need to say anything. Maybe the situation called for him to do something. Since the taxi was crawling along, he utilized the time to call his contacts and find out what advertising agency Ty had landed at. If he couldn't fix what he'd done, at least he could take full responsibility for his actions and apologize.

Five minutes later, he had a phone number to call. When the man answered, Oliver introduced himself but was interrupted before he could explain the reason for his call.

"What do you want?" Sammi's ex demanded, his voice an unfriendly snarl.

For a second Oliver was taken aback. Was this how he sounded when his temper flared? No wonder people tiptoed around him. The image of himself as a boorish tyrant was far from flattering and certainly not one he intended to maintain going forward.

"Sammi said she ran into you at the Adina launch party last night," Oliver began.

"What of it?"

Oliver rubbed his eyes, realizing that keeping a rein on his temper was going to be more challenging than he thought.

"She was upset because you accused her of being responsible for your recent troubles."

"She got me fired." Ty's antagonism came through loud and clear.

"She had nothing to do with it," Oliver assured him, maintaining his composure with difficulty. "I did. Your beef is with me."

"You messed with my career. That's a dick move."

So was the way Ty had treated Sammi, but Oliver held his tongue. He was starting to understand why Sammi had gotten frustrated with his unwillingness to give up his anger and see reason.

"I shouldn't have done that. I'm sorry." Oliver paused to grind his teeth before adopting a conciliatory tone to make it right for the woman he loved. "I'd be grateful if you'd leave Sammi out of it going forward. And if something comes up in the future that I can help you with, don't hesitate to give me a call."

After securing Ty's promise to leave Sammi alone, Oliver's shoulders relaxed. The traffic started moving as Oliver hung up on Sammi's ex. To his astonishment, he felt better now that he'd come clean with Ty. It was as if by taking a positive action to undo some of the harm he'd done, he'd benefited as well. Imagine that. Oliver was grinning as the taxi pulled up to the curb in front of Sammi's building. He paid the driver and got out.

He'd been to Sammi's apartment often enough in the last month for the doormen to recognize him. Oliver nodded in greeting to the one currently on duty and headed for the elevator. As the car ascended, he was surprised by an eruption of butterflies in his stomach. For the last hour or so, he'd been so focused on his cathartic revelations following his visit to the prison that he hadn't considered what he would do if her love for him was well and truly broken.

He knocked on her door and waited in a state of agitation for her to answer. It took so long that he wondered if she peered through the peephole, spied him standing outside her door and walked away. His breath hissed out in relief when he heard the lock disengage. A second later Sammi appeared in the doorway, wearing a fluttery black-and-white polka dot dress and white sneakers.

"How'd lunch with your mom go?" he asked, noting her surprise that he'd remembered.

"You didn't come all this way to ask me that." She scanned his face and then sighed. "It was nice. She's really excited about her new job with the Paulson Agency."

"Can I come in?" he asked, hoping her reluctance wouldn't keep them apart. "I have a lot to tell you."

"I think we said all there was to say last night."

"Not everything," he assured her, recognizing he had a lot of convincing to do. Oliver took her hands in his and gave her fingers a gentle squeeze. "I went to see my father today."

Her gaze lifted to his, fingers tightening ferociously. "How did it go? Are you okay?"

"Don't I look okay?" he teased, her concern the perfect balm for his agitated nerves. He grinned. "Are you ready to let me in so I can tell you what happened?"

She drew him into the apartment and closed the door. Although his attention was focused on her, he noticed an abundance of packing boxes scattered around.

"You're moving?" He didn't dare ask a destination. She'd already removed her toiletries from his bathroom, indicating she'd chosen somewhere besides his place to live.

"My thirty days is up tomorrow." Still holding his hand, she moved into the living room. "What happened when you went to see your father?"

Oliver didn't want to talk about visiting Vernon. He wanted to tell her everything he'd thought about her in the time since. But mostly, he wanted to speak the three words that had been living in his heart for weeks.

"I love you."

For a long moment, she stared at him without comprehension. "What?"

"You are my everything," he said, grabbing her shoulders in a tight grasp. With the floodgates open, declarations and promises poured out of him. "I will do anything to make you happy. Whatever it takes." Realizing his earnest pledges weren't swaying her, he repeated himself. "I love you."

She bit her lip and looked equal parts hopeful and wary. "Since when?"

He wasn't surprised at her resistance. When she'd confessed her love, he'd been unable to say it back. "Since the day you walked into the bar at the Soho Grand. Something happened to me that day, and you've been a part of me ever since."

Sammi was gaping at him with such intensity it seemed as if she'd stopped breathing. He gave her a little shake. She ejected the air from her lungs in an inarticulate squeak.

"But when you asked me to marry you and I said I couldn't unless you loved me—" she jabbed her finger at him "—you said you didn't."

"I never told you I didn't love you," he countered, regretting such foolishness. "I just never told you I did. My only excuse is that I didn't understand what I was feeling was love."

"But you do now?"

"When I met with my father, I realized I was no longer the child who looked up to him. You were right. Letting go of my anger and my resentment was what I needed to recognize that my happiness lies in you. And our baby. You're all I need and want."

Blinking rapidly, she smoothed her hands over his chest while her gaze clung to his in a desperate search for reassurance. "I want to believe that will be enough…"

"Then believe it." Oliver covered her hand where it rested over his heart and brushed his lips over her forehead. "I don't have anything to prove to my father, nor do I need his approval. In fact, I can't believe I wasted so much energy resenting him."

"But the situation with your family isn't over," she murmured. "There's bound to be one event after another that brings up all the old hurts."

"You're right. And I can't promise you that what comes next will be easy, but I know it will be so much harder without you in my life."

* * *

Although these were all the things she'd been dying to hear Oliver say to her, she couldn't quite believe that he'd arrived at such a life-changing transformation in a few short hours.

"And I will be," she promised him. "We're having a baby, after all."

Oliver's brows lowered. "You aren't convinced."

"I am… I mean I want to be."

"Come with me to visit my father." His offer was so adamant that she had no words. "Let's go right now. Come with me and you'll see that there's no more anger inside me for him."

"You were just there," she said. "You don't really want to go back, do you?"

He didn't. She could see it in his eyes, yet he looked resolute.

"I will. And to prove I've let go of the past I'll go every day thereafter if you'll come with me." His voice resonated with earnestness as he continued, "Just like you've come to understand how what happened to your mother has changed the way you view her decisions and actions all these years, I finally understand what you mean. The only way I can stop letting my anger rule me is to let go of past resentment."

"And you're ready to do that." It was less a question than a statement. She could see from his earnest expression that he believed he was ready to move on.

"Going to see him today was the best thing I could've done. I'd built him up to be this figurehead in my mind. A larger-than-life role model for me to look up to. Today, he was behind bars, and all he wanted to do was run me down." Oliver gave a snorting laugh that held only a trace of his old bitterness. "He's the one who's flawed, not me."

"I guess we expected too much from our parents,"

Sammi said, her expression rueful. "They aren't perfect or all knowing, but flawed and driven by fear like anyone else."

Oliver nodded. "If I'd understood that when I was younger, I would've saved myself a whole lot of trouble."

Sammi heard the regret in his voice and desperately wanted to make the hurt go away. "But then you wouldn't have become the man you are. You are a diamond, formed by tremendous pressure and adversity."

"You are the only person in this world who would look at me like a diamond," he said, affection mingling with gratitude in his eyes. "Most everyone else sees me as a pain in the ass."

She touched his cheek, wrapping her love around him. "That's because you have trouble letting people in."

"That's the old me." He flashed his teeth in a bright, enthusiastic grin. "Things are going to be different going forward. I've decided to reach out to both my brothers and fix our relationship. I also need to make peace with my mom. I've been too hard on her, not realizing that she was doing the best she could with what she had." Oliver cupped Sammi's face in his hands and kissed her gently on the lips. "But most important, I promise to be there for you and our baby. Whatever you need. I intend to live up to your trust."

Seeing the determination in his blue eyes, Sammi's doubts receded. She didn't bother asking him if he was sure. One thing she learned about Oliver over the last few weeks was that he never questioned a decision once he made it. She found his decisiveness sexy. Maybe because she had such trouble making up her own mind about things.

"Before we met, I'd never imagined finding someone who made me feel safe," she said, her heart clenching. "You're the only man I've ever truly trusted."

Oliver gathered her against him, and the last bit of stiffness in her muscles eased. She settled against his hard frame with a grateful sigh and slid one arm around his neck, taking reassurance and giving solace.

"Being with you gave me a taste of how wonderful it could be to be a couple, and one day a family, and I'm greedy for more."

When she'd opened the door and spied him standing in the hallway, she never expected to end up in his arms. Moments before he'd arrived, she'd been gearing up to move into the studio apartment alone and suddenly he was stepping forward to confess his love.

Oliver's transformation was a sight to behold. The sweetness she'd glimpsed beneath his sometimes gruff, often wary exterior was on full display at the moment. She hadn't realized how many shadows blocked his soul until they were gone. Awestruck, she basked in the unabashed adoration radiating from his clear blue gaze.

"I love you, Samantha Guzman," he declared, his whole heart in the smile he beamed at her. "Will you marry me?"

Her breath caught. Brilliant joy suffused her whole body. This was the fantasy. The perfect beginning to their family.

"Yes." Sammi's spirits soared. "Oh, yes."

And as Oliver's soft kisses turned demanding, Sammi gave herself over to the thrill of his embrace, ready for anything the future might hold with this man at her side.

* * * * *

COMING SOON!

We really hope you enjoyed reading this book.
If you're looking for more romance, be sure to
head to the shops when new books are
available on

Thursday 15th
October

To see which titles are coming soon, please visit

millsandboon.co.uk/nextmonth

LET'S TALK

Romance

For exclusive extracts, competitions and special offers, find us online:

MILLS & BOON

THE HEART OF ROMANCE

A ROMANCE FOR EVERY KIND OF READER

MODERN

Prepare to be swept off your feet by sophisticated, sexy and seductive heroes, in some of the world's most glamourous and romantic locations, where power and passion collide.
8 stories per month.

HISTORICAL

Escape with historical heroes from time gone by. Whether your passion is for wicked Regency Rakes, muscled Vikings or rugged Highlanders, awaken the romance of the past.
6 stories per month.

MEDICAL

Set your pulse racing with dedicated, delectable doctors in the high-pressure world of medicine, where emotions run high and passion, comfort and love are the best medicine.
6 stories per month.

True Love

Celebrate true love with tender stories of heartfelt romance, from the rush of falling in love to the joy a new baby can bring, and a focus on the emotional heart of a relationship.
8 stories per month.

Desire

Indulge in secrets and scandal, intense drama and plenty of sizzling hot action with powerful and passionate heroes who have it all: wealth, status, good looks…everything but the right woman.
6 stories per month.

HEROES

Experience all the excitement of a gripping thriller, with an intense romance at its heart. Resourceful, true-to-life women and strong, fearless men face danger and desire - a killer combination!
8 stories per month.

DARE

Sensual love stories featuring smart, sassy heroines you'd want as best friend, and compelling intense heroes who are worthy of them.
4 stories per month.

To see which titles are coming soon, please visit

millsandboon.co.uk/nextmonth

JOIN US ON SOCIAL MEDIA!

Stay up to date with our latest releases, author news and gossip, special offers and discounts, and all the behind-the-scenes action from Mills & Boon...

 millsandboon

 millsandboonuk

millsandboon

It might just be true love...

GET YOUR ROMANCE FIX!

MILLS & BOON
— blog —

Get the latest romance news, exclusive author interviews, story extracts and much more!

blog.millsandboon.co.uk

MILLS & BOON

HISTORICAL

Awaken the romance of the past

Escape with historical heroes from time gone by. Whether your passion is for wicked Regency Rakes, muscled Viking warriors or rugged Highlanders, indulge your fantasies and awaken the romance of the past.

MILLS & BOON

MODERN

Power and Passion

Prepare to be swept off your feet by sophisticated, sexy and seductive heroes, in some of the world's most glamourous and romantic locations, where power and passion collide.

MILLS & BOON
HEROES
At Your Service

Experience all the excitement of a
gripping thriller, with an intense romance
at its heart. Resourceful, true-to-life
women and strong, fearless men face
danger and desire - a killer combination!